HEATHER BOYD

BESTSELLING AUTHOR

MISS MAYHEM ✦ BOOK 1

MISS WATSON'S FIRST SCANDAL

MISS MAYHEM SERIES

BOOK 1: MISS WATSON'S FIRST SCANDAL
BOOK 2: MISS GEORGE'S SECOND CHANCE
BOOK 3: MISS RADLEY'S THIRD DARE
BOOK 4: MISS MERTON'S LAST HOPE

Chapter One

<hr>

David Hawke breathed a sigh of relief when the first sign of Brighton came into view through the grimy coach window. He marked his place in the latest K. L. Brahm novel he'd been reading and reluctantly closed the book on the wonderful tale. The journey from London to the seaside resort town appeared to grow longer each year and he longed to already be at his destination, at home in his snug terrace house. If not for his client's witty novel, he would have drowsed the entire way or grown cross with his companion's frequent jostling.

He pressed the heel of his hand against his thigh as impatience clawed at him. He was desperate to stretch his legs, desperate to escape the strangers seated opposite in the mail coach and their assessing glances. He'd dressed a little too finely to be completely ignored by his companions and his seat partner kept reading over his shoulder. Their curiosity compelled him to be vigilant of his possessions and he was weary to the bone.

The coach drew to a stop and he jumped out as quickly as he could manage. He should have hired a chaise for the journey but sitting in the large conveyance alone was a wasteful way to travel in his opinion. He caught his remaining possessions as a groom tossed them down from the carriage rooftop then he set off for his seaside home.

By design, his path took him the long way through the

deserted streets of Brighton just so he might catch a glimpse of the dark waters of the channel before he went to bed. The gentle ocean breeze blew the stench of London from him; the scent of brine cleared his head and cooled his exposed skin. He drew in deep cleansing breaths and a smile broke free. It was good to be home again. He'd missed swimming each morning with his neighbors, if they still came here at this time of year. It had been a long while since he'd had a letter from any of them and he'd come with no illusions they would have time to see him.

But the destination itself still made any uncertainty worthwhile. He'd spent many years here as a boy and his pulse raced at the familiar sights and sounds. Returning each year for a week-long holiday had become a necessary pilgrimage.

After a time, he forced himself away from the water, making his way up Cavendish Place toward his home. Lights burned in the windows of several residences along the street. The Radleys appeared to be here, the Mertons, too. The George's residence was dark and silent but that was not an unusual circumstance. The young Walter George preferred to go out and his sister was rumored to retire early.

He stopped outside the Watson residence, a three-story town house, second from the end of the street. Peter Watson's front door stood beside his own, but their circumstances couldn't be more different. His good mood evaporated. There was one unpleasant matter David needed to take care of for the bank before he could truly settle down to a much needed rest.

The Watson's account was substantially overdrawn with no certainty of further funds arriving to repay the debt. His partner, Knight, had wanted to close the account three months prior. However, David had managed to convince him to wait and give the Watsons more time. Unfortunately, time had run out and he couldn't stall any longer. He had to arrange a meeting with Peter Watson for tomorrow morning. Best to get the unpleasantness over and done with so he could try to enjoy the rest of his stay.

He stepped up to the door. Raucous laughter filtered through a partially open window. Damnation. He'd forgotten it was games night: cards, food, and copious amounts of wine. The fellows from Cavendish Place had likely come to gamble with

Peter Watson, a man who should be saving every penny and pound and not wasting it on Lady Luck. Would it be better to wait until tomorrow to pay his call?

If David had learned one thing in London it was that business came first before fun and friendship. He applied the knocker soundly and waited.

Eventually, the door opened and the Watson's butler squinted at him. "Good Lord, Mr. Hawke. I nearly didn't recognize you. Is everything all right?"

David winced. He'd been dodging the same question from every customer of the bank he'd met with for the past month. The constant enquiries about his health set his teeth on edge. "Of course, Simpson. But I am travel weary." He pulled a card from his pocket. "Would you be so good as to inform Mr. Watson, after his guests have departed, I've come to Brighton and need to speak with him about an urgent matter. I'd like to arrange a meeting with him tomorrow morning if it suits."

Simpson opened the door wide. "Come in, come in, sir. Your friends will be so happy to see you. They were just remarking on your absence from the game, but I knew you wouldn't be able to stay away from Brighton altogether."

David smiled ruefully. "The sea has called to me all year up in dreary London." He crossed the threshold, set his bag aside, and then removed his hat and gloves before handing them to Simpson. He checked his watch. "I assume they are rather bosky by this hour?"

"It *is* growing a touch rowdy, sir," Simpson confessed. "If you'll follow me."

Simpson led David through the Watson residence, an exact mirror image to his own, and stopped before the open doorway to the dining room. Simpson cleared his throat loudly and then announced him.

The room erupted into shouts of welcome and David was engulfed by acquaintances that he hadn't seen for a whole year. Their greetings were so exuberant he had no idea who was speaking at first. When they eventually settled down, he counted heads. Linus Radley, Walter George, and even Valentine Merton had pried himself from his observation of the stars, and they all sat around the table. Peter Watson, the man who owed his bank three thousand pounds, remained seated, cards clutched in his hand and a strained smile spreading across his face.

Watson must realize why he'd come, and all of a sudden David didn't want to think of the notice awaiting delivery inside his bag.

"Join us, Hawke?" Valentine Merton demanded, slapping the tabletop with the flat of a hand.

"Only fools gamble," David replied. "I'll keep my money thank you very much."

"So says the banker," his acquaintances intoned as one then burst into fits of laughter.

"Still as unfunny as it was when I was eighteen and went to work with my father in London." David shook his head, amused they were far deeper in their cups than they had first appeared "Will you never leave off about my chosen career?"

"Well, you were going to be a composer," Walter George accused, his round cheeks shining pink in the candlelight.

Linus Radley chipped Walter's shoulder with a fist. "Wasn't it sculpture?"

Valentine Merton cleared his throat. "No, you are wrong on both counts. Our Hawke was going to be a world renowned painter of beautiful, scantily clad courtesans and actresses were you not?"

That young and carefree man was but a dim memory. "In my salad days perhaps, Val. Painting does not pay the piper. A man must earn his way in the world."

He deliberately kept his gaze from Peter Watson. As far as he could tell, Peter did nothing but chase the next game or other sources of excitement. While their friends had each found employment, a career to make their fortunes from—great or small—Peter appeared to have done nothing productive with his days.

David moved into the room, coming to a stop behind Valentine to observe the game while they recommenced play. As usual, Val was winning.

"Swimming tomorrow?" Val asked, tilting his head back to make eye contact.

David raised an eyebrow. "Is there another way to start the day in Brighton?"

Val twisted in his seat and ran his gaze over David from head to toe. "I thought, perhaps, you might have stayed in to rest. You've lost weight since I saw you last."

It was true, though David didn't like to admit it. He had lost enough weight that his clothes were roomier. His work at the bank demanded long hours and he frequently lost track of time. Meals were snatched when he remembered to be hungry. Aside from that, there was nothing wrong with him. In Brighton he would relax, eat well, and take some exercise.

The sideboard was littered with half-empty platters of food and his growling stomach reminded him he'd barely eaten since breakfast. "Merely lost my puppy fat." He glanced across the room at Walter George. If anything, the younger man's cheeks had grown even more round since last summer. He tipped his head in Walter George's direction. "Unlike some."

"He's swimming with us this year. Becoming quite proficient at it, too." Val leaned closer. "Yesterday, I stopped checking that he hadn't sunk to the bottom."

David chuckled but weariness made it sound false to his own ears. He should go home to dine and catch up with everyone's news in the morning while they swam. He was exhausted but glad to have finally reached his destination.

He cleared his throat. "Gentlemen, I'm afraid I will have to leave you to your game. Merely wanted to let you know I've arrived and pay my respects."

Although they protested he should stay, David waved a hand as he strode to the door.

"Swimming tomorrow?" Peter Watson called loudly before David left the room.

He halted and turned slowly, looking at his friend. Peter appeared anxious—he had every right to be. David forced a smile to his face. "I wouldn't miss it."

When he arrived at the front door, his hat, gloves and his bag had been taken away. He looked for his possessions.

"Good evening, Mr. Hawke."

Chapter Two

The sweet female voice brought a smile to David's lips. He spun about as a tiny young woman, no higher than his chest, stepped from the dimly-lit parlor. "Miss Watson. I did not see you there. How do you do this evening?"

If David had seen her first, he might have been better prepared for her brilliant smile. The young girl he'd watched grow to adulthood was lovely in cream muslin. Soft brown hair matched the calmness of her eyes, delicate sun-touched skin from her days here at the seaside beckoned. Miss Abigail Watson had grown to be a beauty; she fairly took his breath away.

"I'm very well, thank you." She grinned impishly as she turned his hat between her hands. "You did not see me when you arrived, either. I was sitting at the window, looking outside at the comings and goings of Cavendish Place."

He took a pace towards her. His bag sat on a chair behind her. "Were you?"

Her brow creased. "I was beginning to wonder if you were coming this summer."

"I was delayed on bank business." He'd put off his holiday as long as he could because of the Watsons. To give them more time before his business with them wrecked their lives.

Her smile dimmed. "This bank of yours keeps you very busy."

Many of his acquaintances thought he worked too hard and

Abigail's tone was one of deep disapproval, too. However, he enjoyed the back and forth of negotiations too much to stop now. A young woman of her age couldn't understand what drove him. The challenge of making money for his customers brought him immense satisfaction. "One must earn a living, Miss Watson. I cannot neglect the bank's customers. They expect me to do well for them when they give me their funds to invest."

She moved forward. "I hoped to see you when I was in London last month. Does your bank prevent you from seeing friends, too?"

He winced. "You are speaking of your come out? I thank you for the invitation to the party. Unfortunately, the bank required me to . . ."

She waved her free hand to halt his apology. "Yes, yes. I read your letter declining to attend. A very last minute refusal after you had already accepted our invitation. I was looking forward to dancing with you now I am old enough not to look silly doing so."

David frowned. "It wasn't a deliberate snub, Miss Watson. I would have been very happy dancing with you, too. I had to travel north. My business partner fell ill and I had to take his place in some important negotiations at the last minute. I would much rather be among friends than terminating an account."

David bit his tongue. That was exactly what he had come here to arrange this very night and would complete tomorrow morning should circumstances allow it. Miss Watson couldn't know what he'd come to do or she would not be so friendly toward him. "Did you enjoy your time in London?"

Her lips turned up in a sincere smile. "I had a glorious time. London is a very exciting city to visit."

"I think so." Relief coursed through him. She appeared content. David assumed the trip and expense incurred for a London stay had proved fruitful. Whoever he was, he was bound to be made very happy by his marriage to Miss Watson. He cleared his throat. "So, when is the happy day to be?"

"What happy day?"

"Well, I assumed by your smiles you made many new acquaintances in London. Who is the lucky fellow? When will you be married?"

"When someone I like asks me." She set one hand on her hip and scowled at him. "And whoever said I went to London to find a husband anyway?"

David floundered. Why wouldn't Miss Watson be in search of a husband for herself? Every other pretty girl gone up to London ended up some man's wife eventually. "I apologize if I have presumed too much of your intent. Given all the whispered talk of beaus last summer between the young ladies of the place, I assumed you would be keen to marry too and settle into your own home. That is why most young women go up to London, after all."

Miss Watson stamped her foot, proving herself not quite as grown up and serene as her outward appearance made her appear at first glance. "I am *at home*, and don't you dare paint me with the same brush as those grasping ninnies. I don't need to snare myself a London husband. All the men I met there were a bunch of blathering, overdressed fools."

David raised his hands. "Peace, Miss Watson. I didn't mean to offend. However, I find it hard to believe there is not some poor fellow pining for the loss of your company."

She shoved his hat at his chest. David grunted and reached for it, but Miss Watson held onto one side and kept it between them. "Don't think you know me or anything about women, Mr. Hawke. If you had one clue, you'd already be married and better cared for. You're thinner than last year. You've not taken good enough care of yourself since you've been gone."

David groaned. Not her, too. Perhaps he didn't know Miss Watson after all. She hadn't been this forthright last year. In fact, she'd been downright demure when their paths had crossed. He laughed to ease the tension brewing between them. "And who would put up with me? Which poor woman is prepared to be saddled with a boring banker for a husband?" He teased her but David believed he already knew the answer. Very few women would accept his lifestyle—the long work hours, the last minute travel. They would claim his attention as well as his money or they'd go elsewhere for the former, and spend the latter on someone else.

Miss Watson's smile grew. "Wouldn't you like to know?"

Despite years of training to master his emotions in delicate negotiations, David gaped. Had Miss Watson discovered a woman who might hold tender feelings for him? So far he'd not found a woman capable of earning his admiration to stir him from his bachelor state. However, at his age, he probably should consider the matter properly. He would like to hand his wealth to a son one day, but the opportunity to marry hadn't presented itself. Someone nearer to his own age would make life harmonious, as well. He glanced down at the bright-eyed girl before him and ignored the way his chest tightened. "I would indeed, but I suspect you merely tease a crusty old bachelor. I doubt such a person exists."

Her smile grew coy and then she laughed softly. "Perhaps I will tell you, but only if you promise to see out your whole holiday and not run back to London when summoned. A week is barely long enough without cutting it short by two days. We were all very disappointed to discover you'd gone so suddenly without a word last year."

He tugged on his hat as their gazes held, amused that she resisted giving it up. Perhaps Miss Watson had become a touch stubborn in the last year, too. He couldn't remember having such an encounter with her before. "All right, you have me intrigued. I promise not to run back to London this year if you promise in return to impart your important discovery at the end."

"Good, you won't regret it, Mr. Hawke. I promise." Her smile widened to alarming proportions and David feared he had seriously underestimated Miss Watson. He'd just been bested by an eighteen-year-old girl and she'd only used her smiles to do it. He must be getting old.

Eventually, his hat slipped from her fingers. He placed it firmly on his head and tugged his gloves on. "Well, goodnight, Miss Watson. Perhaps we will run into each other again."

"Of course we will." Her brow rose. "You only live next door."

And she only lived here until he evicted her and her brother from their home. The weight on his chest returned, coupled with intense dissatisfaction. He'd delayed as it was, hoping, praying, for her brother to find a way out of his financial mess. If Miss

Watson had not married yet after her time in London then her chances for making one following the foreclosure decreased considerably.

He forced a smile but a chill swept through him. Foreclosing on the Watsons was likely to end any friendship between them. Everyone would blame him and sympathize with the Watsons. No matter what he did, alliances would shift in the next few days as the news of his actions came to light. Regardless of how badly he wanted to find a solution, the problem wasn't his to solve.

David stepped around her to pick up his bag. "Good night, Miss Watson."

"Until tomorrow, Mr. Hawke. Sleep well." She brushed her fingertips against his sleeve in a fleeting caress.

David, foolishly, wished he didn't have to leave her company.

Chapter Three

------◆------

The door closed with a hollow thud behind David Hawke. Abigail lifted her hand to stare at the sealed, thick letter she'd snatched from the top of his travel bag. Stealing was wrong but her conscience warred with her sense of self-preservation. She couldn't blindly stumble forward, waiting for the axe to fall. She knew it was only a matter of time before Hawke and Knight Bank of London called in the outstanding debt.

Her brother's name had been scrawled across the front of the letter in David's strong penmanship and her pulse raced as she ran her fingers over it. The heavy papers had a disquieting air of finality about them.

Although she had tried to prepare herself as best she could these past months, she appreciated that David, and not his business partner Mr. Knight, had come to deliver the bad news. David, their nearest neighbor since she was a child, had seemed sad to be in Brighton again rather than pleased and that spoke well of his character in her mind.

Abigail closed the parlor doors to ensure her privacy. Although Peter would be involved with his friends for hours yet, she didn't want him to accidentally discover her interference. He would be cross and likely embarrassed to learn she'd discovered the situation on her own, but she'd long ago learned Peter wouldn't willingly volunteer information. She had to take matters into her own hands, no matter how unpleasant.

Her hands trembled as she moved toward the candelabra on the pianoforte. She had little time to familiarize herself with the terms of David's letter or make plans for the future. Peter would never think to do so.

The seal was thick and she broke it after a struggle. David's, not his business partner's, cover note was tersely worded. Her brother had thirty days to provide the bank with three thousand pounds or the bank would seize the Watson's assets and that meant the house she stood in. They'd be cast out onto the street, and worse, Peter may have to enter debtor's prison. She glanced around and tears filled her eyes. Abigail loved her parents' house. She loved living in Brighton near her friends.

Her legs wobbled and she sank onto the pianoforte stool, raising the letter to fan herself. How could she bear to leave Cavendish Place? How could Peter have let this happen to them?

Oh, she wasn't so foolish to have no idea. It wasn't in Peter's nature to think too far beyond the next day. She loved him but his pigheaded obstinacy drove her to distraction more often than not, which was why, at her friend's urging she had taken a more active role in the running of his home. If left to him, they would have nothing to eat each night, no coal to burn during the winter. She had developed a sneaky habit of reading his letters just to find out what the next catastrophe would likely be.

She folded the letter carefully.

Hopefully, David would think he had merely misplaced the missive and she could return it without him noticing. She felt very bad for deceiving him in this way. He had always been kind to her, even willing to speak to a girl much younger than him in past years. But she was older now and not prone to patience.

A fierce blush swept over her cheeks and she fanned herself again. She had been forward in her speech with David tonight. Much more so than usual, yet he hadn't grown colder with her. He had seemed puzzled.

Puzzled could be good. Puzzled could distract him from meeting with her brother and discussing the lack of payments. Abigail pressed a hand to her hot cheek and giggled. Who was she kidding? She had only momentarily startled the man with her bold suggestion that he needed a wife to take better care of him. David had a single-mindedness about him that had intimidated many of the local girls to cancel their plans to bring him up to scratch. He wouldn't forget about the debt, or be swept away by the mere idea of finding a bride. Abigail had to think of something else, something to change her fate and her brother's quickly.

She nibbled on her fingertip. They had nothing valuable enough to sell that could cover a debt of this scale. Although she peeked inside David's bag to obtain the letter, she hadn't the cold-blooded ruthlessness for a life of thievery, which left her precisely where she was now—reliant on Peter's skills with cards. Where might a needy person in Brighton acquire funds at short notice?

There must be something she'd overlooked. Maybe if she talked the matter over with Peter they could find a solution together.

Immediately, Abigail shied away from that notion. Peter did not discuss anything with her. If she was going to avoid eviction in thirty days she needed to talk to a friend with a healthy dose of good sense. Luckily, Abigail had such a woman was close at hand.

She stuffed the letter into her pocket and snatched up her shawl. She could sneak from the house to visit Imogen George tonight without Peter being any the wiser. Her best friend's house was next door, one house closer to the water, and she wouldn't object to a visit at this hour.

Getting out of the house undetected by way of the rear door proved easy enough given the noise Peter and his friends made. The servants had all gone off to bed, and the walled gardens were dark and silent. But, just in case anyone was as restless as she, Abigail clung to the shadows and moved silently through the wilting vegetable patch.

The summer had been harsh and the scant grass crunched under her slippers. She quietly unlatched the rear garden gate and peered into the lane. Her heart raced, hoping no one lurked in the deep shadows. She quickly shut it behind her and then ran for the safety of Imogen's rear garden. When she shut Imogen's gate behind her, she pressed her hand to her belly to steady herself.

Perhaps she was getting too old to be sneaking out of the house alone. Imogen did it all the time. Somehow Abigail never seemed to manage it without her nerves being overcome. But she was desperate tonight. She needed sensible advice.

Striving to calm herself, she hurried to the George's rear door and knocked. The housekeeper smiled kindly when she recognized Abigail and let her in. "Miss Imogen is in the front parlor as usual," the woman said.

"Thank you, Mrs. Perkins."

Abigail stepped through the dark house and stopped at the open parlor door, peering into the moonlit room. "Imogen?"

"Abigail!" Imogen exclaimed. "Thank goodness you've come. I've been worried sick all evening."

"Why? What have I done now?"

Imogen clucked her tongue. "Oh, you know exactly what the problem is. I saw Mr. Hawke arrive. He stopped at your house first. Was it terrible?"

Now that her eyes had adjusted to the meager light, she saw Imogen seated near the window, peering out into the street. Abigail crossed the room. "How funny. We were both spying on our neighbors again."

"Well, I had nothing else to do with my evening. I finished my book a little while before Mr. Hawke strutted up the street."

Abigail sank into a chair opposite her friend. "Mr. Hawke does not strut and you know it. Why are you suddenly so against him? Last year you thought him nice enough and entrusted your inheritance into his keeping."

"Given recent events I'm reconsidering my decision. Friends should overlook debts if they want to keep people as friends. I've a mind to withdraw my funds and find another banker."

"Don't be foolish. Mr. Hawke is an honest man." Abigail sighed and drew out the letter she'd stolen. "It's a lot of money, Imogen. More than Peter could hope to win in a year. Mr. Hawke has been very good, he's given us a month before we are evicted, but what can I do? I don't want to leave Cavendish Place."

Imogen patted her hand but didn't take the offered letter.

"You are pretty enough to have the option of marrying anyone you choose to avoid the unpleasantness of eviction. If no one else catches your fancy, my brother would take you on without a word of protest. He has funds enough to save even your brother."

Abigail laughed. Marrying pudgy Walter George was out of the question. It would be like marrying a brother. She felt nothing for him except a limp friendship. No, Walter George wasn't the man for her.

Imogen shrugged and glanced out the window as someone passed by on their way toward the sea shore. "I know he may not seem much to look at but he would be kind to you."

Abigail, feeling guilty for her laughter, covered her friend's hand. "Walter is a nice man, a very good man, too, but I simply couldn't put us both through that horror. I wouldn't make him happy. I want to marry someone who loves me. Desperately, if possible."

"I know." Imogen glanced at her lap and pleated her gown with her fingers. "I feel the same about loveless marriages as you. I just don't want you to leave Cavendish Place. If you married Walter we could be sisters and never be parted."

Abigail's eyes widened as a solution occurred to her. "Sisters! That's it. Imogen, have I ever told you that you are a true genius?" She threw her arms about her friend in gratitude and hugged her. "I need to find my brother a wife. An heiress, in fact, and I know the perfect one."

A frown crossed Imogen's face as Abigail released her. "The only heiress you know is Miss Melanie Merton. Would you really want to live under the same roof as that woman?"

Imogen did have a point about Melanie. The reigning beauty of their circle possessed the largest dowry and could be very demanding of those around her. Peter had never shown any interest in Melanie, but he might if given enough encouragement. Wasn't having him marry a harridan better than him losing everything?

She smoothed her hands over her gown. "There is no one else unless another comes to Brighton."

Imogen's expression grew skeptical. "The last man who called at Merton House to propose practically ran away afterward. Have you come to dislike your brother?"

Abigail sat up straighter. "I love my brother. I'm doing this for his own good. Starting tomorrow I shall somehow engineer meetings between them. Who knows, maybe Peter will come around with her dowry to sweeten the deal."

"You've become very mercenary about this business, Abigail. Almost as bad as Miss Radley." Imogen squeezed her hands. "I'm not sure I like your sudden turn of practicality. Where has your romantic heart disappeared to?"

"I can be romantic after I save my brother from ruin," Abigail said. "And this is nothing at all like Julia Radley's wild schemes, thank you very much."

"I hear she's set her cap on Hawke this year. I wonder if she'll succeed."

Abigail was not unduly alarmed by the news. For the past three years, she had been regaled with wild plots of how one or the other of her friends thought to snare David Hawke for their own when they came of age. He had a presence that drew the eye, even if he never used it to his advantage. He was a wealthy man, too, which made his bachelor status so much more interesting to her friends. So far none of them had succeeded in catching him and Abigail couldn't imagine Julia's brash outgoing personality would suit him at all.

"Well, whatever happens, I hope someone does choose Julia and soon. I love her dearly, but she'll have no reputation left, or anyone to marry, the way she challenges the boys at every turn." Abigail jumped to her feet as another tall shape sauntered past the window. "I think the game has ended. Mr. Radley is headed for home. I'd better return before Peter discovers I've slipped out of the house without a word to anyone."

She kissed her friend's cheek and groped her way through the dark house for the rear entrance. Why Imogen liked the dark so much escaped her. Abigail could never manage without a candle. When she reached the rear steps, she drew in a deep breath and squared her shoulders. Peter would marry an heiress and be saved. She just had to ensure he and Melanie Merton could be thrown together as much as possible.

She hurried down the garden path and let herself out the rear gate. As she latched it, the sound of a boot scraping over hard earth to her right, between her and her own garden gate, reached her ears. She jumped as a large dark shape detached from the wall and moved toward her.

Panicked, Abigail fumbled with Imogen's gate, but she couldn't open it again. When she turned to face the stranger as he came into view, her heart pounded in fear.

Chapter Four

David Hawke appeared out of the black shadows. Abigail's heart restarted. She collapsed against the gate and sucked in the air she desperately needed. There was no danger. It was just David out for a midnight stroll.

"I've been waiting for you, Miss Watson." David's voice was a soft, dangerous growl.

Abigail backed up a step in shock. "Really? Why?"

He moved closer. "When you were a little girl I turned a blind eye when the fruit on our trees mysteriously disappeared overnight, only to appear again from your kitchen. My mother was very put out, but I held my tongue because I didn't want to stir up trouble between our families. In this instance; however, I cannot be so forgiving."

She swallowed the lump that threatened to clog her throat. "I haven't taken anything from your garden in years."

David glanced left and right as footsteps echoed in the night. He caught her arm to drag her into the shadows cast by her rear garden wall. "Do not play games with me, Miss Watson. I know you've taken a letter from my luggage and I demand it be returned forthwith."

He tightened his hand and she gasped at the strength of his grip. "Please, Mr. Hawke—David." She struggled against his hold. "Not yet. I have a plan to fix this but I need a little more time."

"Well, if thievery is part of your grand plan then my reluctance to become involved was in vain. What were you thinking?" He shook her a little. Startled, she set her hands on his chest as he drew her closer against him. It was a shock to be caught in David's embrace. As she had observed before, he was so much bigger and warmer than she had imagined a man could be.

The clean scent of his cologne filled her senses and she peeked up through her lashes. His eyes were dark as he glared down at her. This was not the David Hawke she knew. This was a stranger and he utterly overwhelmed her.

His tight grip eased. "You should not have become involved in the matter, Miss Watson. There is nothing you can do. Your brother is a fool to take you into his confidence and to worry you unnecessarily."

Abigail gulped. "Peter tells me nothing. I worked it out for myself."

"You're reading his correspondence? Women cannot help but meddle," he grumbled. "Do you understand how bad the situation truly is? I have had to plead, cajole and insist my partner give Peter more time so you might never know how close to ruin you were. But it's been all for nothing."

She nodded. It was very much in David's nature to try to shield those less fortunate than himself from discomfort. She appreciated his attempt but discovering the truth was better than living in ignorance. "I've known for months and I could not stand to wait for the decision. I knew you had to make one soon."

David released her. "I'm sorry. Your time in London must have been tarnished by the situation. I wish you had found a husband to take you away from the mess. The matter cannot be forgotten, but Peter refuses to deal with the bank. He's ignored my partner's letters and I've come in person to settle the issue."

Abigail captured David's large hand and squeezed it. "If there was an advantageous marriage in the making, Peter would have additional funds at his disposal soon and he could keep the property. The bank will get its money in the end."

He eased closer as he stared down at her. He gripped her hand in return. "Has he a sweetheart?"

"Not exactly," Abigail hedged. "But he will have soon enough. If he proposes marriage, can the bank wait until he has her dowry?"

David nodded. "Only if there is a date set and the woman's dowry is sufficient to clear all the debts. My partner at the bank should be satisfied with that."

"Thank you. Thank you. You truly are a good friend to us." Abigail released David's hand and then threw her arms around him. She hugged him tightly. He was wonderful to allow them the additional time to settle the debt. Impulsively, she stretched up on her toes and kissed him.

Unfortunately, her first-ever kiss was brief because David reared back as if she'd struck him. He gaped at her, eyebrows raised in a shocked awareness of her scandalous behavior. "Why did you do that?"

Abigail crashed back to earth as the enormity of her actions struck her. *I've kissed a man.* The extremely wealthy and unattached banker, who had, when she was very young, rescued her from the clutches of his backyard tree. Heat swept over her neck and face. She turned away. "I'm sorry."

After a painfully long silence, David cleared his throat. "Miss Watson," he began. But then he cleared his throat again and started over. "Miss Watson, do not believe actions of that kind will sway me from carrying out my duties should your brother not marry after all. You will only hurt your pride and likely ruin your reputation in the process."

Abigail pressed her hands to her face as his words drove home how unaffected he was by her first kiss. Of all the foolish things to have done this might have been her finest folly. She may never be able to look at him without blushing again.

After a time, he patted her shoulder. "I know these are troubling times. You're confused and grateful for the reprieve I've given, but flirting with me will not help in the end. Watson must marry a woman of wealth, or you must both leave the property by month's end."

She nodded. "I understand."

"We will not speak of this matter again, or to Watson about the theft. May I have my letter returned to me?"

Abigail drew the papers from her pocket and held the envelope out. Her hand shook as David took it from her and slipped it into his own pocket. "You'd best return indoors." His tone had gentled to a soft rumble, exactly how he had been all her life. All trace of his anger and disappointment had vanished.

She looked up at him. David *was* normally a civilized, reserved man, the sort you compared others to and found them wanting. Her stomach tumbled with uncertainty, her throat closed as she wished she'd done a better job of kissing him the first time. It had been her first after all, but she hadn't planned it well enough. It wasn't exactly the kind dreams were made of. She certainly hadn't done it to sway him from his plans.

He tilted his head to the side, silently observing her. Her stomach tumbled again and warmth filled her chest. David was so very handsome in his impeccable London fashions. Glossy black boots, tight fitting black trousers, and burgundy striped waistcoat, beneath a black coat. He had always drawn her eye and she felt surprisingly safe whilst alone in his company. Despite the circumstances, she was pleased he had followed after her tonight rather than confront her brother about her behavior. Now that he wasn't angry could she claim a proper kiss—just for practice of course—without David speaking of it, too?

Bravely, she caught the lapels of his elegant coat. The wool was smooth against her bare fingers and she pulled him down to her level, as she had once seen a woman do on the seashore with her beau, and pressed her lips against his firmly. For a moment, David froze and she feared he would draw away again. But then he skimmed her mouth with his in a delicate dance that took her breath away. He cradled her face gently with a hand as his lips molded hers to his purpose, sucking at her lips each time they parted. She sighed at how lovely he was being about indulging her. She hadn't even had to ask.

His tongue fluttered across her lips and she leaned into him.

Unfortunately, David drew back at that moment and she almost fell at his feet. He regarded her warily, his breathing rough and loud in the night. "Did you not listen to me?"

Her body hummed with delightful tremors, and Abigail nodded as she set her hand to the gate to support herself.

"Gracious! Kissing can make the heart race, can't it?" she whispered, pressing her fingers to her lips. "I listened. But thank heavens I ignored what you said."

He folded his arms over his chest, his expression stern. "I do not like the game you are playing, Miss Watson. You will only be disappointed. This business will not go away because of a few rash kisses bestowed."

Abigail lowered her fingers. She might have enjoyed kissing David, but he didn't appear at all pleased. She sighed, disappointed not to have made a better impression. "Mr. Hawke, I had no sinister motives in kissing you. It was my first, but since you appear to dislike kissing me, I'll not continue. I shall say goodnight to you. My curiosity has been satisfied about kissing— at least for now."

She shut the gate behind her and cast a quick glance in his direction. In the moonlight, he looked infinitely more dangerous than the crusty bachelor he claimed to be. To Abigail's way of thinking, the gate wouldn't prove much of a barrier should he wish to launch himself over it. Her heart fluttered at the idea.

"First?" He stepped up to the gate and clenched the top. "Miss Watson, I fear my own curiosity has not fared so well in the exchange. Do not tempt me further."

She set her hand to her hip boldly. "Or what?"

He smiled. "Wouldn't you like to know?"

He disappeared in the blink of an eye, leaving Abigail with the rush of exhilaration coursing through her veins and a burning curiosity to know what it would take to tempt him into another kiss.

Chapter Five

The cool brine of the channel supported David as he floated with the calm waves in the early morning light. This was what he'd missed most while living in London. There, he never had more than a copper tub of water to submerge in and it lacked the slight itch of salt on his skin. He scrubbed his hands over his arms, enjoying the way his skin tingled.

Around him, his friends employed their own style of sea bathing, but Walter George was certainly a distraction. Despite Valentine's assurance last night that Walter's swimming had improved, their youngest companion had sputtered a great deal at the edge of their swimming party. David had been at the point of suggesting he go ashore when everyone else stilled to float along with the current.

The first to leave the water was Valentine. He never stayed in long, preferring to rush his dip and then hurry back out again. Given the hours Val kept with his study of the constellations, he'd be keen to return to bed so he would be fresher for the evening's celestial studies.

Walter George followed him, grasping for a length of towel as soon as his feet hit the sand. He covered his less-than-muscular physique quickly. Modesty among men tended to slip at the seaside. David liked to dry off naked in the sun and gain a bit of color. Today his skin seemed pasty white in comparison to the others who had been swimming here every day for the past month. It had been a long time since he had been so active or outside for so long and he was feeling slightly unsteady.

He flipped over and made his way ashore, stumbling a little as his feet readjusted to walking on the sea floor. He had grown soft in London. Brighton would toughen him up. It always did. He sat next to his clothes, a few feet from where Valentine lazed, sunning himself, and wiped his face dry. "Beautiful morning."

"Beautiful evening, too." Val dragged his gaze from the sunlit heavens. "I saw a surprising new constellation last night. One I never imagined to see."

David grinned. "That's wonderful. But if you've made a discovery why have you not shouted it for all to hear this morning? You must tell everyone."

Valentine scowled. "It wasn't that kind of constellation. Not the kind that thrills my blood. I could have sworn I saw the shape of a Hawke swooping on tender prey. I thought better of you, old man."

David stilled. Had his friend seen those rash kisses between him and Miss Watson? Val's scowl convinced David he had.

"It was a mistake and will not happen again," David quickly assured him.

Valentine lifted his gaze to the heavens and sighed. "If it does, I will expect to hear a suitably grand announcement and to receive an invitation to the wedding. Lips do not usually connect so accidentally. She's a good girl, or has been until now. I would hate to see her heart broken when you disappear back to London."

Guilt made David squirm. He'd spent many hours since last night debating the wisdom of having allowed the second kiss from Miss Watson. Sadly, he couldn't erase the memory of her from his mind. Saying Abigail had been enthusiastic had been a vast understatement. He'd never experienced such a sweet, soul-consuming kiss. He'd quite forgotten himself in the rush of discovery. She'd surprised him with her flirtatious comments, too. She wasn't the girl next door he knew or expected to speak with.

Despite those imprudent kisses, he shouldn't, couldn't offer for her. She was too young. Far too young for an old man like him, and his business with her brother would set them at odds. It could not be halted by any sort of attachment developing between them. He was a fool to even entertain the brief fantasy.

Regardless of still being wet, David threw his shirt over his head, raked his fingers through his hair, and gazed out at the shapes bobbing with the waves. Peter Watson had drifted further out than usual, effectively avoiding any possibility of conversation. David hadn't really wanted to spoil the morning with bank business himself, but he couldn't put it off indefinitely. They would have to talk, and Peter would be made to listen in the end.

He dressed, thinking over how to begin the discussion. He didn't hold out much hope to remain friends after this. But he did hope not to become bitter enemies.

Val slapped his shoulder. "Must have been some kiss."

"Beg your pardon?"

"That kiss last night. You've not been yourself all morning. Are you in love with the girl?"

"Not at all." But he did feel oddly protective of her. Despite how it looked, he didn't want Val to misunderstand the situation. David had confided in Val before when he'd been faced with a troubling situation, and frankly, he could use an impartial opinion. He moved closer to his friend so he couldn't be overheard. "I can explain. By chance I spotted Miss Watson rush out her back gate late last night. I was concerned because she was unattended. I knew Watson had you all for company and likely wouldn't notice she had left the house. I followed her up the laneway, and she called on Miss George. Rather than leave, I waited until she came back out."

Val set his hands on his hips, his expression amused. "And just how did the kiss come about? You tripped and your lips stuck together?"

David still couldn't work out that part. But it appeared Val didn't know there had been two and he wasn't going to ask which one he'd seen if he could avoid it. "This is rather embarrassing. Apparently, the lady wanted her very first kiss to be from someone she knew. I swear I have been nothing but respectful with her and will continue to be so."

Val frowned. "You called at the Watson's first last night before you even crossed your own threshold. Why?"

"I had some business to take care of with Watson. Since he had guests, that business is still outstanding and preys on my mind today, not the kiss with Miss Watson. I have no designs on his sister. None at all."

It was only half true. He might think about the sweetness of her lips, but he wouldn't act on those thoughts. Yet, it did feel very good to confide in someone he could trust not to spread harmful gossip about Miss Watson.

Val chuckled and broke the comfortable silence. "So, is she the first of the young ladies to throw herself at you? They're all on the hunt for a husband now and think we're easy targets for practicing upon. You'll grow used to it by the end of the week and learn to move quicker unless you wish to be trapped. Were you really surprised?"

He drew in a deep breath as his tension dissipated. He wasn't the only one to stumble into such a situation and come out utterly befuddled by the experience. "Could have knocked me down with a feather."

"It shouldn't have. They're all testing their wings these days so be careful. You're wealthy, not too bad looking, and probably considered quite a catch."

David punched Val's arm.

"All joking aside, even Miss Radley is fluttering her lashes at the oddest moments," Val continued. "Once, she did it so often I thought she had a spec of dirt in her eye and asked her if she required aid. The look I got could have made me a eunuch. But out of all the fellows in Brighton, you're possibly the one man Miss Watson is most comfortable around so be cautious of her unless you wish for a shackle about your leg."

A warm glow built in David's chest but he quickly repressed the sensation. "Don't be ridiculous. I'm too old for her."

"You were always coming to her rescue when she was small." Val chuckled. "Remember the time she followed us to the seashore one morning? Everyone except you had their trousers about their knees or off before we realized she'd watched us disrobe."

"Please don't remind me." David covered his face at the memory. "Her questions on the way home burned my ears. I have always hoped she wouldn't remember seeing your skinny backside disappearing into the waves."

Valentine punched his arm. "Well, she's seen all of us and not done a thing about it. There is just your backside to satisfy her curiosity about."

"That isn't likely to happen."

Valentine stopped suddenly. "Do you know how many proposals of marriage she's turned down? Three. She's getting a reputation for breaking hearts."

David's mind grasped onto the idea. A speedy marriage for Miss Watson would solve one half of the problem. She'd be spared the pain of eviction and have a home of her own to go to. "Why did she refuse her suitors?"

"Who knows why women do anything. What I thought were perfectly sane, intelligent young ladies two years ago have turned into simpering and fluttering creatures while our backs were turned." Val shuddered. "I warn you, Brighton has become a dangerous playground for the unwary gentleman."

"Miss Watson doesn't simper or flutter. She's rather direct actually." David's face heated. His defense of her indicated he had given Abigail considerable thought. He avoided meeting Val's gaze. "She mentioned overdressed young men in London with a great deal of distain. I am surprised to find her unattached after her time in London. She should have done well."

Val glanced at his clothing and grinned. "If she has no care for fashion then perhaps I might just prove good enough to be acceptable, even with my skinny backside."

David regarded his friend, a sense of discomfort prickling along his spine. Valentine would be considered a good catch, not wealthy but well off, only somewhat eccentric with his nightly stargazing habits. It was probably time he considered taking a wife.

They stopped in front of Valentine's home. If David could encourage a match between Valentine and Miss Watson then he might not feel so dispirited about what he had to do. However, he wouldn't like to force two people together when there was an inequality of feeling. "A man should never propose unless he means to change his life, but Miss Watson is sensible and could be good for you. She'd be worth the expense."

"So says the banker," Valentine intoned. "I am amazed such sentimentality and romantic notions run through your head."

David rolled his eyes. "You may laugh at me now, but I've had my share of gentlemen clients bitterly complain about the expense of family, and particularly wives who married them for position and money rather than affection. Romantic or not, marriage is not a decision to rush into."

"The expense of a wife shouldn't be a problem for you then, would it? You may be as romantic as you please and choose from any number of lovely ladies. However, your situation is unique. You have no family to appease when making the decision on who to wed." Valentine sighed dramatically. "I must gain approval from three women before even contemplating such a decision. It must be nice to come and go at your leisure without having someone to answer to if you are tardy, messy or absent altogether. I'm not keen to add another lady to my household."

"Neither am I," David said but as he spoke he acknowledged to himself that he wasn't being entirely truthful.

Valentine glanced sideways at him. "Your business is doing well, I trust?"

"Yes, business is booming. A family would never understand the demands of my work," he muttered the last softly. In a sense, it was good he had not married. If he had, he'd likely endure years of discord because of his devotion to work.

"Well, you shan't ever know for sure until you have a family of your own," Valentine warned sagely. Valentine said his goodbyes, reminding him of the Radley dinner tonight, and David walked up the street alone. He glanced at the Watson's front window as he passed by. The curtain twitched, and his pulse tripled. Yet he did not want to give Miss Watson further encouragement so he hurried to his own door and closed it swiftly behind him. He would keep a greater distance from Miss Watson, deal only with her brother from now on, and ensure he was never in a position to kiss her again.

He climbed the stairs for his bedchamber in order to wash and change for the day. Once there, he peeled his clothes from his body and sat on the edge of the bed. Bone deep tiredness tugged at his limbs and his eyes stung. He rubbed at them impatiently. He had much to do and couldn't indulge in the luxury of returning to slumber, but the soft familiar feather bed cradled him with such comfort that he rolled onto his side and pulled the covers over his head.

Chapter Six

◆

Abigail allowed the parlor curtain to fall back into place with a heavy sigh as night descended on another perfect Brighton day. David Hawke had not reappeared since this morning. His front door remained stubbornly closed despite her wish to see him and have the notice calling in the debt delivered to Peter.

She glanced to where her brother paced, hands restlessly shuffling cards, making them dance in the air as he performed tricks. Peter, too, had been surreptitiously peeking out onto Cavendish Place all day, but not even he had mentioned what time David was expected to call. She couldn't believe David had changed his mind about delivering the letter. Once he made a decision, he stuck to it. It was one of the things Abigail admired about him.

Once her brother had the notice, and was suitably desperate about the situation, Abigail would broach the subject of a union with Miss Merton as a solution to eviction and debtor's prison. Surely Peter would see the logic of the match and fall in with her plans for him to marry. There really was no other choice.

Peter's pocket watch clicked as he snapped it closed. "Well, it's time we stepped out. Are you ready, little sister?"

"I have been ready for an hour, as you well know. How sad I'm always ready ahead of time, and you must rush about."

Peter grinned. "Now, now. No need to ring a peal over my

head. I did not see the moth hole in my waistcoat and I did change when you demanded it. I'm ready and fit to be seen, am I not?"

She glanced over him with a critical eye. At her urging, especially in light of the damaged waistcoat, he'd returned upstairs to dress a little more formally than he would normally. It wouldn't do to be lax about his attire while courting an heiress. Abigail would have to sneak into his bedchamber and inspect his other clothes for similar damage.

Tonight, his cravat was perfectly tied for a change, his hair was neatly styled, and his pocket watch chain gleamed in the candlelight. Given the effort he had made with his outward appearance, she hoped Melanie Merton would finally notice what a fine man he was to look at. Only time would tell.

Although the evening was fair, she picked up her best shawl, placed it around her shoulders, and then linked her arm through Peter's. "I've been looking forward to dining with everyone tonight. Melanie is so lovely, but I rarely see her unless it's at a dinner somewhere."

Peter's brow rose as he opened the door to lead her out onto Cavendish Place. "Last week you complained that Miss Merton kept standing in your way when you were talking. Why the devil are you keen to spend time in her company?"

Abigail shook her head, glancing quickly at the front of David's house. Every window was as dark as if he had not come to Brighton after all. Where was he? "I was mistaken in thinking it deliberate. She's so elegant and tall, and I so short, I suspect she didn't see me."

Peter led her down the street, away from David's house. "Strangely charitable. You have forgotten I saw it all. Damned rude of her to interrupt your conversation with Radley. If she does it again, I will say something cutting about it this time."

Abigail dragged him to a halt. "Don't you dare say one unkind word to Melanie. Not now."

"Why not now?" Peter's eyebrows shot up. "Abigail, I won't have you slighted like that again. I don't care if I offend the silly chit or her family. She has no right to lord her fat dowry over you as if you were beneath her notice. It isn't money that makes someone a better person. It is how they treat others."

Abigail set her free hand to her trembling stomach and prayed Melanie might be in a friendlier mood tonight than she usually was. She simply had to see Peter's better qualities. She was sure the right woman could overcome his interest in gambling.

Her brother rapped on the Radley's door and they were whisked inside the elegant townhouse.

Mr. Linus Radley greeted them warmly. "Watson. Miss Watson. So happy you could come."

"Thank you, Radley." Peter shook hands with him and then headed for where the gentlemen had clustered on the far side of the drawing room.

Mr. Radley smiled at Abigail. "You look as lovely as ever, Miss Watson."

A happy warmth invaded her chest at the compliment. She had dithered over her gown, settling on a cream silk edged with heavy burgundy embroidery. It had been a favorite since her time in London. "Thank you, sir."

She glanced into the room, noting who had come. All the ladies of their group were here and of the men, David would be the last to arrive.

Mr. Radley cleared his throat. "Do you have a moment, Miss Watson? There is a pressing matter I wish to discuss with you."

Abigail stilled at the memory of the last time someone had spoken those exact same phrases to her. Surely Mr. Radley was not so ridiculous as to propose marriage to her, too. She gathered her courage and pasted a smile on her face. "Of course. What can I help you with?"

He leaned closer. "I need to obtain your support in regard to my sister."

Relief trickled through her and she relaxed. "What has Julia done now?"

Mr. Radley's heavy sigh raised the hair on her neck. "She intends to challenge the gentlemen to a swimming race. I've done all I can to dissuade her, but she is determined to ignore the impropriety of mixed bathing to prove she's a strong swimmer. You have as much influence on her as anyone. Can you try to convince her it's a very bad idea?"

Abigail blushed as she remembered the unclad state the gentlemen swam in. Accidentally catching half of them stark naked was a memory she strove to push from her mind. Thankfully, Mr. Radley had not been there that day or she really would be blushing now. "You give me too much credit, sir. Julia has always gone her own way. But I will try."

"That is all I can hope for." He stood silently at her side, gazing across the room to where the ladies sat, an expression of disappointment on his face.

Uncomfortable with remaining apart from the group for too long and wary of giving the wrong impression about their discussion, she cleared her throat to recapture his attention. "I should like to join the ladies now if there is nothing else you wish to speak of, Mr. Radley."

He startled as if he *had* forgotten she was standing at his side. "Yes, I'm sorry to have detained you. Do try to convince her if you have the opportunity. I fear what will happen to her reputation—and the family's—if word spreads of her intentions."

"Of course." Abigail made her way into the parlor where Imogen, Julia Radley, Teresa and Melanie Merton sat. "Good evening, ladies."

While the other greetings were warm and heartfelt, a shrill 'Miss Watson' was all Melanie Merton offered. The sharp edge to the salutation sent a chill through her as did the cold gaze that raked her from top to toe. Determined to advance Peter's cause, she braced herself to overlook the rude behavior and improve their friendship. A bit of harmless flattery couldn't hurt. "Miss Merton, you look lovely this evening."

Melanie preened a little. "Thank you."

When Melanie made no attempt to return the compliment or continue conversing, Abigail glanced about. Julia and Imogen gaped at her until she began to wonder if she'd left half her hair hanging down her back.

"Dinner is served," the Radley's butler intoned, saving them from the need to make further small talk. They all stood, Melanie taking the lead to proceed into dinner. Imogen caught Abigail's arm when she would have followed. "I may just be sick to my stomach before the evening is through."

"Oh, Imogen. An advantageous marriage is the only way to save Peter."

Her friend frowned as she glanced around. "Well, I hope you can live with the consequences. Has Mr. Hawke spoken to your brother yet?"

That feeling of disquiet raced through her again when she thought of David's darkened house. "I don't believe so. He did not call at the house to see Peter today."

"I overheard we may have odd numbers for dinner. Melanie will talk of nothing else for a month if that is the case."

Abigail worried at her fingertip briefly. "Did David decline the invitation?"

One of Imogen's eyebrows rose. "They say he never answered it. No one has seen him since the men went sea bathing this morning."

Abigail took her place beside Valentine Merton at the table and participated in the general dinner conversation, but her thoughts remained on the man she had kissed by moonlight last night. Had David taken ill after the swim? Was he all alone in his dark town house? That thought didn't rest easy with her. Shouldn't someone check to see if he were well?

Chapter Seven

David groaned and rolled onto his side as his stomach bitterly complained it was empty. Pale light pierced the gloom through the gaps around his bedchamber drapes and he fumbled for his pocket watch. The hands showed eight o'clock had just passed. He must have dozed off for a few minutes.

He crawled out of bed, stretched his aching limbs, and peeked outside. The sunny day had turned dreary with rain. He frowned as he parted the drapes wider. There hadn't been a cloud in the sky when he'd been swimming this morning. The swift change in the weather surprised him. He'd been asleep less than an hour.

Bemused, he scratched his head, noting that salt had stiffened his hair until it stood on end, and looked for his discarded clothing. But although he searched, everything he'd left on the chair next to the wardrobe was gone. His housekeeper must have crept in and taken them to wash while he'd been napping. Odd, given that Mrs. Lynch had never come into his bedchamber before while he was in it. He didn't care for the idea. He'd only been asleep for a short time.

When footsteps approached, tapping lightly up the stairs, he dived back into bed and pulled the covers up his chest so he wouldn't shock the poor woman. Mrs. Lynch only came in to clean in the mornings and to set a pot on to cook during the day. He had no need of a full-time servant. Not for one week a year.

He saw a breakfast tray first, and then his eyes widened as Abigail Watson's face peeked through the gap, only to quickly vanish again.

Horrified, David sat higher against the headboard and yanked the covers all the way up to his shoulders to cover his nakedness. "What on earth are you doing here, Miss Watson?"

"I was worried about you. May I come in?"

David's body tensed, everywhere, at that idea and he quickly tamped down such improper thoughts about his innocent neighbor. "No, you may not. I'm not decent. Go home, Miss Watson."

There was a long silence from the hall, and then Abigail muttered to herself. "Not particularly friendly in the mornings. Must remember that."

Regardless of his request that she leave, Abigail entered his room carrying a breakfast tray. The smell of ham, chocolate and fresh baked cake came with her and his empty stomach tumbled over itself loudly.

She approached and set the tray over his thighs, a bright blush making her cheeks rosy in the half light, her smile timid. "It is good to see you finally awake. I feared a physician would be needed."

He pulled the tray higher, attempting to hide the effect her nearness had on his body. "Miss Watson, what are you talking about?"

As she opened the drapes a touch more and then faced him, he noted the apron tied around her waist and her small bare hands fumbling with the material. "It's Monday. You've been asleep since yesterday morning as far as your housekeeper and I can determine."

"Monday?" David stared at her in shock and then picked up his pocket watch again. The hands hadn't moved since he'd last looked at it. "What time is it?"

She lifted a chair and relocated it close to the bed. "A little after two o'clock in the afternoon. I've never heard of someone sleeping so long unless they were gravely ill."

Her concern touched him. "I'm not ill."

A frown crossed her face as she sat. "So you say. But most

people don't lie as still as a corpse either, ignoring young women creeping into their bedchamber."

She appeared so worried he forgave her for the impropriety of invading his home. However, no one else would if they discovered she was here. "You were here while I was sleeping? Is Peter with you?"

"No. Peter does not know I'm here. I begged your housekeeper to let me check you were still breathing as she was too afraid to come near you."

She twisted her hands in her lap, reminding him the girl should be sent away for her own good, although it was likely far too late to save her reputation. Someone may have seen her enter his bachelor household. They would make the wrong assumption about her presence and any talk would ruin her. She had to leave. "Mrs. Lynch," he bellowed.

"She cannot hear you. Mrs. Lynch needed to visit her sister in Hove urgently and I gave her permission to go since you were still asleep. I told her our housekeeper would watch over you in her place. Of course, my housekeeper knows none of this."

David shook his head. "Miss Watson—Abigail. What of your reputation? What were you thinking to invade a bachelor residence? If word of this gets out, there will be hell to pay."

She'd have no choice but to marry him and that wasn't what he wanted for her. Abigail deserved a choice in who she wed.

"I was thinking someone I considered a friend might need someone to look after him," she said softly. "Your breakfast is growing cold."

David glanced down at the overflowing tray. He couldn't deny he was starving. To sleep even half as long as he had was unusual for him and his stomach protested the lack of nourishment. He'd eat first and then see Abigail returned home and deal with whatever consequences befell them later. He glanced at the tray and at her apron again.

"I promise my cooking will not harm you. Peter suffers it well enough when I can convince Mrs. Simpson to let me into the kitchen."

David groaned at the thought of Abigail slaving over a hot oven on his behalf. That was not the life she should have. She should be pampered not put to work. How could he possibly repay her kindness and concern? Words were his only choice for now. "Thank you, Miss Watson. I may sound churlish and severe about you being in my home and unchaperoned, but I do appreciate your efforts. I just hope we can return you to your house before you are discovered."

He attacked the plate, savoring each bite as he tried to adjust to the lost time. He couldn't believe he'd been quite that tired as to sleep through an entire day, a night, and half another day. Abigail perched on the edge of her chair. She studied him, or rather stared at him, eyes wider than he'd ever seen them. When he glanced down, he realized his sheet had fallen, exposing his bare chest to her innocent eyes. He jerked it back up again and tucked it under his arms. "This is delicious but if you're not going to leave, I'll need a shirt or robe to put on."

Young women would not be used to seeing so much of a man. He was surprised she hadn't fled but then she had seen naked men before, albeit at a distance when she'd followed her brother to the beach. Hopefully, she didn't remember much of that. Unfortunately, he couldn't get out of bed to cover himself decently. He hadn't a stitch of clothing on and he didn't want to shock her if she saw any more of his skin at close range.

"Of course, you must be cold." She bounced up from her chair and flung his wardrobe doors wide.

Actually, he wasn't in the least bit cold. David's pulse raced and his body burned with unaccustomed heat. Keeping hidden how she affected him proved difficult. He'd never imagined Abigail might sneak into his house—or any man's house—for that matter. He'd always thought her rather proper and restrained until the day before yesterday. What else about her had changed during the last year?

She stood before his wardrobe, her fingers sliding over his clothing as she searched for what he'd requested. When her hand passed over his robe twice, he cleared his throat. "That's my robe on the right."

She jumped and quickly acquired the garment, but then she lifted the material to her nose as she turned. Her gaze flickered over his body and he tensed again at the odd expression in her gaze. As she drew closer, her bold appraisal added to the torture. How much more of this he could stand before he pulled her into his bed he didn't know, but it was imperative that she leave. Now. Before he dragged her against him and completed her education on kissing and expanded her understanding of male anatomy.

She held out the robe. "I have a problem."

David had one, too. His attraction to Abigail was an unforeseen complication to his life which would make calling in Peter Watson's debt that much harder. He quickly settled the material around him, belted it at the waist and repositioned the tray to cover his aching privates. "Oh?"

"I have no idea how to convince my brother to marry."

David picked up a piece of cake and bit into it as he considered how to answer. "There is an old saying that you can lead a horse to water but you cannot make him drink," he said eventually.

Abigail slumped back in her chair. "Exactly. I can dangle many pretty girls beneath his nose, but bringing him to the point of proposing is beyond my experience."

David frowned. "Forgive me for being indelicate, but I had recently heard you'd had experience with marriage proposals. Three wasn't it?"

Her eyebrow arched. "Who told you about my suitors?"

"Mr. Merton mentioned them yesterday. He saw you—us—in the lane the other night."

A bright blush swept over her cheeks. "Did he threaten to tell my brother?"

"Surprisingly, no. However, I did promise him no further mistakes would be made."

Her nose wrinkled quite adorably as she frowned. "And I've ruined that for you today by coming here unescorted. Never mind that now." Her expression turned thoughtful. "The proposals I received were a surprise to me. I did nothing to bring them about. One fellow asked me immediately after our first dance. I'd never met him before that night so I was taken aback by the abruptness."

"And the next?" David took a second bite into the seed cake, cursing himself for asking about her suitors in the first place.

Who had asked her for her hand in marriage would gain him nothing but prolong her time in his house.

"By letter. Anonymously."

David choked on the cake and coughed to clear his throat. He reached for the tea and swallowed some. "How on earth could the fellow have expected you to accept if he didn't identify himself?"

She chuckled. "That was my first thought, too. I didn't meet with him at the arranged time and place."

"I should hope not," David bit out savagely. What if she had gone? What fiend might have been lying in wait for the innocent woman? "What does your brother say about this?"

"I think my brother prefers to forget I'm of marriageable age."

Damn, but Peter Watson was a fool. He should be keeping better watch over her than this. "And the third?"

"The very first actually, and it was awkward to say the least."

Full to the brim, David set the tray aside and repositioned himself in the bed. He was still aroused, but he could listen to Miss Watson talk all day and never tire of hearing her confidences. "And who was that?"

She clenched her hands together. "Walter George."

"Ah, perhaps not the young man for you."

She twisted her hands together. "I felt so bad for refusing. Imogen and I are the best of friends but Walter is . . ."

He laughed at her inability to describe their rather staid neighbor. "Walter."

She threw both hands up in the air. "Exactly. He's not dashing or heroic. He's pleasant but unexciting," she complained softly.

Miss Watson had clearly spent some time determining what she didn't want in a suitor. What she *might* want intrigued him. "And you require excitement?" David scrubbed at the stubble on his jaw and grimaced at how rough he must appear. "I imagine dashing off to suitor number two's rendezvous could have proved an adventure."

Her brow rose haughtily. "That would depend on your definition of excitement."

Chapter Eight

David spluttered at her bold answer, unable to believe the direction their conversation had taken. Never in a million years had he thought of engaging in banter of this nature with his innocent young neighbor. He leaned forward, eager for her next response. "There's more than one?"

Her eyes sparkled with mischief. "In my experience, yes."

David stifled a laugh as he sat back. Quite a bit had altered in the last year and in Abigail's case the changes were rather pleasing. "I still find it hard to remember you're all grown up. Sometimes I still think of you sneaking apples from our tree, your long hair tangled in the branches."

"I haven't been that young or naïve in quite a while." Abigail stood and reached beyond him, stretching to grab the tray he'd set aside. Because of her position, her bottom was enticingly displayed before him.

The image of young Abigail Watson was banished forever, replaced by the siren leaning over his lap. He clenched the sheet and groaned. "And other times I can barely think. Abigail, take yourself out of my house before I do something we will both regret."

She lifted the tray, her smile serene and unaffected by his warning as she lingered at the bedside. "I still need your help, but if you think better with clothes on, I'll await you downstairs in the parlor."

If he stripped Abigail of her clothes, and dragged her into his bed, she'd understand his predicament and state of mind. "That would be appreciated."

"Oh, and David. What could you possibly do that would give me any regrets?" She disappeared quickly, leaving him with the compelling desire to chase after her to show her exactly what game she'd started by coming into a bachelor's home alone. He wasn't so old that he didn't know how to seduce a woman if he set his mind to it. However, for the present he was undecided about the wisdom of such an action. Given what he knew of Abigail now, he wasn't sure who'd be seducing whom.

He listened to her retreating footsteps and breathed a sigh of relief to have behaved as a gentleman despite the temptation. Abigail had taken too great a risk with her reputation by coming here, by not leaving a partially covered man as soon as she discovered him awake. Honor demanded he do the right thing by her, not seduce her. That meant sneaking her out of his house before she was discovered, and, if they were found out, ensuring they married immediately.

He swung his legs over the side of the bed, and hoped he and Abigail didn't have to marry because of necessity. In his experience, that sort of union was never a happy one. No matter how the circumstance came about, both parties were often plagued by doubts and insecurities.

For David, he could imagine a life with Abigail's honey-soft lips molded to his, her lithe body pressed against him. Conversation, too, would be worth the time spent. He'd always enjoyed their short talks. But he lived in London and worked a great deal. She'd be miserable as his wife.

He stripped off his robe and dressed in record time, ignoring the stubble darkening his jaw for the present. The sooner he answered her questions, the quicker she could leave. He'd deal with everything else later if action became necessary.

He rushed down the stairs and barreled into the parlor. Abigail had made herself at home, slippers abandoned, feet curled beside her on the sofa. She'd removed the apron but had not restored her gloves to her hands. To see her arranged so contentedly on his furniture made him wish he were not quite so honorable. After a moment, her cheeks turned a startling shade of red and she scrambled to put the slippers back on. "That was quick. Peter takes an age to dress."

"I had a pressing need to hurry."

She smiled, and David did his best to convince himself her look was one she might bestow on a favorite uncle. Full of trust. However, he didn't deserve her trust. He longed to scoop her up in his arms and taste her lips again. He sat in a chair opposite, far enough away that he couldn't take liberties if the opportunity presented itself. He would treat her as a customer of the bank and not as a pretty young woman with incredibly tempting curves. "Right then, what exactly do you need help with?"

She folded her hands in her lap. "I'd like to know what would make a man propose marriage."

David rubbed his hand over his mouth to hide a smile. "Miss Watson, I've never proposed marriage before so I wouldn't know how to answer that."

Her frown returned and he was still smitten. "Well, I had guessed that. You're unmarried which I find quite ridiculous. But, if you should one day consider it, what might prompt you to go down on bended knee? Theoretically, of course."

David laughed. The conversation was simply too absurd. He'd been woken by an adorable virgin, fed, and now questioned about how he would acquire a theoretical future wife. Did Abigail not understand the danger she was in? Dowered or not, a man of lesser character would have tossed her over his shoulder and made her his already. Instead, she waited patiently with her hands folded in her lap. Perhaps she didn't consider him a catch for marriage after all, and the growing attraction between them was all in his imagination. "First off, I'd want to know we had something in common."

"Like a love of Brighton?" she asked.

He studied her. What could he and Abigail possibly have in common? There was eight years between them in age. He knew her to be generous to those she could help, loyal but occasionally untruthful. However, she'd appeared utterly contrite when he'd caught her the other night and given the impending eviction, he couldn't hold snooping against her. "Hmm, not so much the attractions of Brighton alone, more the style of living that would come with being married to me."

Could she bear to leave Brighton and all her friends behind if they had to marry? Would she really be miserable in London as his wife?

Her head bobbed enthusiastically. "That shouldn't be a problem. Peter is an amiable man. What else?"

"I'd have to like the woman."

Her chin dipped and she raised a fingertip to her mouth. "Can you make someone like you even when they didn't to begin with?"

David regarded her warily. Abigail had always held a special place in his heart. He'd never had a sister and he'd watched her grow with a certain kind of pride. However, his feelings for her now were certainly not brotherly. Did she realize that? "It happens all the time, of course. Sometimes people pretend affection to obtain the alliance, but the problem with that is they never know the real you and often don't enjoy the later discovery. Miss Watson, are you trying to pair your brother with a woman who does not care for him? You will do him no favors if you are."

"She could come to love him," she declared boldly.

Her sweet face held so much hope that he wanted to reassure her instantly. But he disliked giving anyone false hope. What she wanted might not be possible. "Miss Watson, you cannot force love and attraction. It simply is there, or it's not." After all, what had sprung up between them had caught him by surprise—proof that his own words held more than a grain of truth.

A harsh knock sounded on the door and Abigail gasped. "Someone is here."

"Obviously," David murmured. He stood, caught her hand and pulled her from the sofa. "You need to hide. Quietly now, lets not make too much sound and see if your reputation can be salvaged."

She clutched his hand tightly. Her warm brown gaze rose to his and his breath caught. "But we haven't finished talking," she whispered.

Her grip changed, and she stroked his thumb with hers.

David stared at her, feeling altogether besieged by stirrings he shouldn't acknowledge. "Miss Watson, are you here to ask my help to find Peter a wife, or were you hoping to secure a rich husband for yourself by any means—even compromise?"

Abigail had the grace to blush. "I wouldn't do that to you."

Yet she still didn't release him.

He tugged until their hands parted. "But here you are, unchaperoned, in a bachelor's household with no apparent intentions of leaving. It appears very odd to say you are not looking to be wed when your actions suggest you are."

"I'll hide. We can talk another time," she murmured, and then hurried down the hall.

Although he regretted what he had to do, David steered her toward the hall closet far away from the front door. Abigail wrinkled her nose, but then she looked up and quickly brushed her fingers through his hair. Her touch was soft and stirred him beyond words.

"It's still a bit messy from your long sleep," she whispered.

Her bare fingers brushed his ear, and then his jaw as she caressed him. The urge to kiss her rose again.

David quickly shut the door in her face. What was he going to do with her? She couldn't go five minutes without shocking the hell out of him and he was on the verge of doing something extremely wrong. He raked his fingers through his hair to finish her work as he approached the door.

A quick glance through the peep hole showed Peter Watson standing on the top step. Of all the rotten luck. He couldn't risk inviting Peter into the house in case Abigail revealed herself accidentally. The discussion about the debt would have to wait yet again. David glanced over his shoulder to make sure Abigail remained hidden before he opened his front door. "Mr. Watson, what a surprise."

Peter frowned, glancing past David's shoulder. "Is this a bad time?"

The worst in living memory. David set the tip of his boot behind the door just in case he was dealing with an angry brother who knew his sister was as good as ruined and planned to barge in and throttle him. "Actually, it is."

"Ah. Well. Here." Watson thrust an envelope at him. "My sister suggested we invite you to dine tomorrow night."

David took the envelope, a small ripple of unease curling through him. He would now have the opportunity to speak privately with Peter, but Abigail's dinner would be spoiled because of it. "That is very kind of her. Of you both. I'd be honored to attend."

Watson shuffled his feet, clearly uncomfortable with his errand. "Well, we will see you tomorrow."

"See you tomorrow." David closed the door on Peter slowly, and waited 'till he'd returned to his own house before rejoining Miss Watson down the hall. However, the closet was empty when he opened the door.

When he checked the house, Abigail had vanished as if she'd never been there at all.

Chapter Nine

———◆———

Abigail threw herself over Imogen's bed and covered her face with both hands. "I am in so much trouble."

Imogen, seated at her desk by the window, calmly packed away her papers before patting Abigail's head. "I take it Mr. Hawke has delivered his bad news."

She lifted her head from the counterpane. "No, he hasn't spoken to Peter. The wait may be killing me, but it is so much worse than that." David's bad news paled in comparison to her situation. She had made a terrible mistake and had no idea what to do to rectify the situation. Abigail rolled over and stared at the square white ceiling above her, wishing she could hide from the truth. She was a wicked, wanton woman who couldn't control her riotous imagination. Visions of yesterday's visit to David Hawke's house wouldn't leave her. Another blush heated her cheeks as she remembered the sight of him propped up in his wide bed, and the brief flashes of his bare skin made her breath catch even now.

Imogen sat next to her. "Then you haven't spoken to Peter about marriage to Miss Merton?"

Abigail shook her head. "Not yet. I haven't had an opportunity."

"Well I cannot say I'm disappointed," her friend told her. "Your brother could do far better than to marry a woman who'd make him miserable with every word she uttered. I've never known anyone to be so disagreeable so often. Is there anything she does like?"

"I do hope so." Abigail fidgeted. Miss Merton's exacting nature was a considerable hurdle to overcome. "Otherwise I don't know what else I'll do. It seems like the only choice now."

Imogen clasped her hand tightly. "Peter will find a way out, I'm sure. He always manages to land on his feet. But is that the only matter of concern? You seem more troubled than I've ever seen you."

Abigail drew in a deep breath. She had been bursting to tell Imogen about her encounters with David since the moment they had happened. But she'd never felt so confused before. Kissing David was both desirable and wrong. He'd made it very plain he wasn't interested in sharing further kisses. "I kissed David Hawke the night he arrived in Brighton."

Imogen's sharp intake of breath made her wince. "And you waited 'till now to tell me?"

Abigail covered her hot face with her hands. "Actually, the kiss was a few days ago and I was embarrassed. I am still embarrassed," she mumbled. Not exactly true but close enough. The embarrassment stemmed mainly from her wish for further kisses and David's reluctance to grant them.

Imogen pulled Abigail's hands away from her face so she couldn't hide, her brow creased with concern. "Embarrassed? Why? Was it ghastly? Does he have foul breath?"

"No, the exact opposite of ghastly." Abigail closed her eyes, remembering the slight rasp of his evening whiskers against her lips. Yesterday morning he'd looked so handsomely disheveled, his jaw so dark with new growth that she'd had to touch, she couldn't not think about him every moment since. She covered her eyes to block out the memory. But it was no use. He had managed to replace every foolish fantasy she'd ever entertained about men. "He kisses very well. However, I do not believe David would agree with me. He didn't appear happy afterward."

"Well, the nerve of him." Imogen grew an inch in height, full of righteous indignation. "I hope you can put the incident from your mind. There are many men with better manners."

If only words could expunge her wickedness. "Imogen, I'm

afraid there is more," Abigail said softly. Better to get the whole truth out before she lost her courage. Imogen would never tell and could be counted on to offer sound guidance.

"Oh dear, have you made a fool of yourself over him?" Imogen hurried to the door, peeked out, and then closed it fully to give them privacy. When she returned, she gave Abigail's hand a squeeze. "Did you expect him to propose because of a single kiss? I know for a fact that gentlemen place little importance on a girl's first kiss. As long as no one sees, they never think of it again."

"Two kisses. But the lack of proposal is not what concerns me. I never thought he would look at me in that way. He's much too grand." She shook her head again. "However, I went to his house yesterday." And she hadn't been able to stop thinking of returning to see more of David Hawke since: his broad shoulders, his muscular arms, his utterly devastating smile when he laughed. He made her feel completely different than usual and she had no idea what to do about it or him.

"Abigail," Imogen cried out. "Are you all right? Did he impose on you?"

"Of course I am all right," Abigail groaned. "Why would you imagine I wouldn't be? Mr. Hawke is a gentleman."

Far too much of a gentleman, in fact. He'd had ample opportunity to kiss her, touch her, and had not taken advantage of the situation. It had been decidedly lowering to be so unable to stir him to the same passion he inflicted on her senses while she couldn't seem to behave properly in his presence.

"Not much of a gentleman to have kissed you and not proposed." Imogen pinched the bridge of her nose. "Now, because you are such an innocent in the ways of men, I want you to explain to me exactly what happened between you both. I'll force his hand toward matrimony if he's led you astray."

Panic rose in Abigail's chest. "Don't you dare do such a thing. He did nothing wrong. I was worried about him," she said, her voice softening on the last. She squared her shoulders. "No one could recall seeing David since he went swimming on Sunday morning. By Monday morning I was concerned and went to call on his housekeeper. She said he was still abed and complained he'd not bothered to eat the meal she'd prepared the day before.

The moment his breath drifted over my finger while he slept brought tears of relief to my eyes. I've never known someone to sleep so soundly. He didn't stir except to breathe."

"But, Abigail, he can take care of himself and always has," Imogen said sternly. "You should not have risked your reputation like that."

"That was exactly what he said, but I'd like to know who does worry for him," she demanded. Poor David had no one else that she could see. "Certainly not his housekeeper. None of his friends, our brothers, called at his house this morning to inquire about his absence."

Imogen sighed again. "You were watching his house all day? Oh, of course you were. You were waiting for him to call on Peter to deliver the letter."

She nodded. Another half truth.

"I know I must forget the kisses with David, and I will in time." Heat swept Abigail's cheeks. "But the waiting is killing me and I have had enough. I've arranged a dinner and invited David to attend tonight to speed along the process of bringing the matter of the debt into the open."

"Are you sure that is a wise thing to do? Peter may not appreciate your meddling in his affairs."

Abigail shrugged. "I love my brother, but I know his faults well. He will wait until the last moment and then everything will be in a panic. The best thing to do is discuss the matter as rational adults, explain the benefits of a prudent marriage, and hope he sees sense. Will you come?"

"Your brother will not like having a witness overhear any part of the conversation between himself and Hawke," Imogen warned. "He will be embarrassed if he discovers I'm aware of the problems he faces. What if the gentlemen argue?"

Abigail took a deep breath. "I need a fourth to make the dinner even and I'm also hoping your presence will prevent any words from spilling over into unpleasantness. Please, Imogen. I only ask because I know you can keep a secret."

Along with keeping the men civil, Imogen would distract her from staring at David's lips all night. How could she look at him over the dinner table without remembering him nearly naked and undressing him with her eyes? The evening could very well be a disaster if she blushed and stammered that he was the most beautiful man she had ever met. At least Imogen could be counted on to kick her under the table if she was struck dumb by him.

"All right, but don't expect me to have any influence on either gentleman," Imogen said eventually. "They always do as they wish in my opinion. Eight o'clock?"

"Thank you. I knew I could count on you." She gave Imogen a long hug and then fell back on the mattress. "With you there tonight I'm sure the evening will end well. Peter would never raise his voice in front of you."

"Don't be surprised if he does." Imogen stood. "At least I'll be on hand to prevent any further kisses from occurring between you and Mr. Hawke. I won't leave you alone with him for even a moment. Now, how about we take a walk? All this fretting over David and Peter is very bad for you. The fresh sea air will clear your head."

Abigail allowed Imogen to pull her to her feet and they made slow progress toward the channel. Although Imogen meant well by her words, they disappointed Abigail. She'd been secretly hoping for another opportunity to speak privately with David about Peter's future marriage. She was hoping he'd come up with an idea to encourage the match between her brother and Miss Merton because Abigail couldn't think of one. And if they were alone, and kisses were in the offing, would it be entirely bad if she tasted David just once more?

"Imogen," Abigail began. "How is it you've become such an authority on men?"

A small smile twisted her friend's lips. "Believe me, it wasn't planned."

Abigail caught Imogen's arm. "Come on. I told you my secrets. It's about time you shared yours."

Imogen was the closest thing to an older sister and she felt a little cheated to be excluded from her secrets.

Her friend sighed. "Very well. I fell in love a long time ago, but it didn't last or lead to anything more."

"But why not? You're lovely."

"The gentleman's thoughts and mine didn't align. I thought I had found the love of my life and planned to marry him but he thought he'd found a naïve and willing girl to warm his bed for the summer."

"That's terrible." Abigail stopped. "What happened? *When* did this happen?"

"Two summers ago." They let a carriage pass and then continued on for the seashore. "When I discovered my error, and his plans, I made sure the gentleman walked with a distinct limp for a little while."

"You did what Peter warned me to do if ever I was importuned."

Imogen nodded. "I've considered thanking him for the suggestion, but that could lead to questions I'd rather not answer. Since then, I've made a study of the men of our acquaintance. They really are simple creatures. A suggestion of pleasure or a favorite treat can often be the perfect lure to get what you want from them."

Abigail sighed. So far she had failed to tempt David into doing what she wanted. He did exactly as he pleased. "David Hawke is not like that."

"Hawke is exactly like that. So is your brother, by the way. Men each have desires that drive them and those needs can be fulfilled if you are brave enough to tempt them the right way. However, you must be careful because marriage is not at the forefront of their thinking. Everything else decadent is."

"Imogen," Abigail began with a sinking feeling in the pit of her stomach. Had Imogen gone too far and been ruined? Was that why her opinion of men was so low? "Have you ever been *very* brave when it comes to men?"

"In my opinion, a lady should never admit to her own ruin." Imogen stared out to sea, her gaze thoughtful and serious. "However, the answer is no. I've never found a man who could tempt me to throw my principles aside so completely for the sake of a little passion. Mind you, I'm not adverse to the idea where there is love involved. Yet circumstances and my nature make me doubt I could ever be so foolish as to trust my heart to any man unless it was for the deepest bonds of affection."

Chapter Ten

David leaned back in his chair, listening to the familiar tick of the ormolu mantle clock and the silence of his Brighton house. The stillness bothered him a great deal today. He'd gone out earlier to visit Mrs. Wiggins, an old acquaintance of his mother's, to offer his condolences on her husband's death. But their time together had only reminded him of the barren emptiness of his home life. During his visit, Mrs. Wiggins' two daughters had called, young ones clinging to their skirts.

Her questions about his solitary state and lack of children had been excruciatingly direct. He'd actually blushed and stammered like a younger man would when embarrassed because the image of a likely wife and children were remarkably like Abigail Watson in appearance. It didn't help that Mrs. Wiggins had mentioned Abigail in passing at least a dozen times. He'd had no idea his neighbor had become fast friends with the woman.

Since his return, he'd given in to the urge to check he was alone in the house, and not about to be besieged by Abigail. It was ridiculous to think she might come back. Although he hoped she would not risk her reputation again just to speak to him, a part of him looked forward to it. He would see her at dinner tonight, with actual chaperones this time, but he had no further insights to share on how to make Peter Watson—or any man— propose marriage to a woman if he didn't want her for his wife.

He tucked away his folder of notes, the topmost of which was Miss George's banking statement, disturbed by his lack of focus. He'd meet with Miss George and her brother tomorrow afternoon, well ahead of his departure for London, and hopefully discuss investment opportunities for the next year. Miss George should be pleased with the state of her investments. However, after the Watsons were served with their notice, he had doubts he'd remain as banker to the Georges.

However much as it tickled him to know Miss George was the celebrated and much read author, K.L. Brahms, as a customer of his bank, she surely wouldn't remain so. A pity. Miss George's writing really was wonderful and he enjoyed getting his hands on each new story before anyone else. Aside from him, and her editor, she demanded the matter was to be kept secret. He'd not even shared the real identity of K.L. Brahms with his business partner and he hoped whoever replaced him would share the same scruples of discretion. Society would be scandalized to know the darling of literary circles was not in fact a man but a very young spinster.

David picked up the tea tray, deposited it in the kitchen, and then strolled out of the house to look up at the sky. The day hadn't turned out particularly pleasant. Grey clouds clustered above him so he couldn't venture too far from home without risking becoming uncomfortably wet. The only bright spot on his horizon was tonight's dinner.

A small whimper reached his ears and he looked about the garden for the source. Huddled by the wall of his garden, between wilted radishes and sad cabbage heads, sat a small ball of filthy brown fluff. Bedraggled, trembling, small beady black eyes stared at him and a black nose sniffed the air. A puppy? He glanced about but the poor thing was entirely alone.

He crept closer. Animals never really warmed to him, but its forlorn whimpers touched him. He leaned down to scratch its damp head. The little beast wagged its tail hesitantly. As he stroked the tips of its ears the speed of its wagging increased. Encouraged, he carefully eased his hand beneath the puppy and lifted it away from the vegetables so he could get a better look. Four very muddy paws scrambled in the air for purchase just as the sky opened up and hard rain fell.

Startled by the rain and sudden wriggling, David drew it against his chest and hurried toward the shelter of the house before they were both drenched through to the skin. He stepped into the warm, and thankfully, empty kitchen, uncertain of what he should do with the beast. Its whimpers and struggles pulled at his heart. Cleaning and drying it off seemed a necessary first step. He dropped the pup onto the battered work table and peered at him. Or was *he* a *she*?

The little beast shivered, dropping spots of mud onto the clean surface, and made to return to him. David pushed it back to the middle, but kept a restraining hand on it this time. Poor creature. What a sorry state to be in, all mud and misery; all alone in the world, just as he was.

He dragged his handkerchief from his pocket and wiped ineffectually at the muck and water around its dark eyes. However, the handkerchief proved no match for the mud caked to its paws. He'd barely made a dent before he realized a thorough dunking and scrub would be called for to make the beast in any way presentable.

"You, sir or madam whichever you may be, are not fit for decent company," he said out loud as he struggled out of his coat and ruined waistcoat.

The puppy's ears flattened at his tone and David rubbed them until the beast perked up again. He rolled up his sleeves in between petting the pup, leaving smears of mud on the white cotton shirt. Resigned to the ruin of his attire because of one small creature, he peered about the kitchen, searching for what he would need to save the rest of his wardrobe. He wrapped the animal in a rag he spied hanging from a chair and tucked the pup tight against him while he organized a bucket of warm soapy water.

He chatted to the pup as he worked and by the time he had readied the bath the animal had fallen fast asleep against his chest. He felt cruel to wake it, but it couldn't remain as it was. Not if it wanted to enjoy more of his attention. He carefully unwrapped the rag from the animal and slowly lowered it into the bucket.

The pup did not enjoy the bath at all; especially the repeated scrubbing and dunking required for cleaning. However, the drying seemed to improve its mood as did the combing to a degree. The odd snarl had the pup nipping at his fingers and he grew more careful as he brushed through the short coat. In the process of cleaning, he discovered he held a pure white pup, a terrier of some description, and a female. "So, you are a lady, eh?" The pup burrowed under his hand in search of more attention. "How much trouble will you be for me, princess?"

By the end of the chore, David was tempted to keep her. How much trouble could a pup be? The only thing that worried him was the hours the pup could spend alone at his London apartment and the fuss that might be raised if he were to take her with him to the office. How could he possibly entertain the idea of keeping an animal that would demand all his spare time and then some? He couldn't very well rush out into the park every hour to let it tend its business. Regretfully, he concluded that he'd have to find someone to care for it, someone living here in Brighton would be best.

He found Princess—for that's what he decided to name her—something she seemed to enjoy eating and when she would take no more nourishment, he carried her upstairs to his bedchamber while he dressed for dinner with the Watsons. He dragged an old, sturdy traveling trunk out from under the bed and placed bed linens inside. Given the sides were quite high, the pup should be safely contained while he changed. The pup walked around in circles sniffing her new bed, curled into a ball with a whimper, and then promptly fell asleep.

Hopefully, she would sleep all night or at least until he returned from dinner.

David turned back to his wardrobe and changed as quietly as he could. When he was satisfied he was dressed well enough to call upon the Watsons, he picked up the pup, trunk and all, and quietly took her back to the kitchen being careful not to jostle her about too much.

Once he was sure Princess remained asleep he eased out of the room and let himself out the front door and locked it behind him. David took a large steadying breath. It was just a friendly dinner with the most beguiling Abigail Watson, followed by a possibly hostile interview with her brother. He patted the letter in his pocket while his heart grew heavy. The time had come. He would deliver the demand for payment at the very end of the evening. With luck, Abigail would not become distressed should her brother turn surly.

Chapter Eleven

---◆---

Acting as hostess for Peter's friends had never bothered Abigail very much before, but tonight her nerves were a jangled mess. She wanted everything to be perfect when David arrived. The flowers on the table were low enough to prove no barrier to conversation; the menu was simple and should prove a success.

"Abigail, if you move that accursed vase one more time I'll toss it out the window," Peter grumbled from the doorway. "What's gotten into you?"

David was coming and she was anxious to see him. Her visit to his house had stirred up all sorts of mischief, especially her thoughts about the future. She liked David a great deal more than she'd first realized. She'd had a brief idea that climbing into bed with him and snuggling up against his broad bare chest would not be a very terrible thing to do before she was married. The idea was rather intriguing. That sort of thought rarely occurred to her around other men. But the memory of his bare chest, the fine hairs disappearing beneath the tumbled sheet had set her heart to racing repeatedly since that moment.

He was much more muscular and imposing without clothes than she'd imagined a man could be. In fact, she'd had to keep her hands clenched on her lap to control her curiosity.

Imogen cleared her throat, alerting Abigail that she'd been staring off into space and hadn't answered her brother. "I want the evening to be perfect, that's all."

He stared at her hard. "Why is tonight different than any other? You don't usually go to this much trouble. It's just Hawke, not the king, coming to dine."

"And I have never hosted a dinner for him before," Abigail snapped. "You've likely forgotten, but I have behaved exactly this way before entertaining any of our friends for the first time."

Imogen slipped into the room, her gaze darting between them anxiously. "For heaven's sake, Mr. Watson, don't bother her. Ladies like to have everything just so. Men, however, will leave everything to chance and pot luck and let the sensible run the gauntlet of their misadventures."

Peter's eyes widened as he stared at Imogen. "I know that saying. Do you read K.L. Brahms?"

Imogen shrugged. "Of course, doesn't everyone with sense?"

He rubbed his jaw. "Well, I suppose most of my acquaintances would, but I would have thought the material somewhat broad and, perhaps a trifle vulgar, for a woman your age."

"Vulgar?" Imogen laughed and turned away, covering her mouth. "They are subjects one hears spoken of everyday. How can the truth be vulgar?"

"Yes, but surely your brother doesn't approve of you reading that man's work," Peter continued.

Imogen turned and the look she leveled at Peter should have sent him scurrying. Abigail sighed. Peter should know better than to lecture Imogen. She would do exactly as she pleased regardless of his opinion. Abigail quickly stepped between them. "Perhaps what my brother thinks on the subject of K.L. Brahms could be kept for discussion until after we dine."

A throat cleared at the door and Simpson showed David in.

He smiled warily. "Am I interrupting?"

Abigail's breath caught. A blush heated her cheeks as she stared across the room's expanse. David's London finery filled the space so completely he made her brother's attire seem terribly shabby and outdated.

"David. I mean Mr. Hawke. We didn't hear your knock." She rushed forward to welcome him with a slightly unsteady curtsey. He was so handsome. His smile as he bowed made her heart tumble over quite alarmingly. It was all she could do to remain still.

"So it would seem." He turned to Imogen. "For the record, Miss George, my favorite K.L. Brahms title is *The Mischievous Miss*. Very witty. I recommend it to all my clients in need of a book to cheer them."

Imogen's smile widened. "It's very difficult for me to admit to a favorite. I love them all," she boasted.

It was terrible to be the only one in the room with no idea what they were talking about. Peter would not allow her to read the author's books without his permission. The K.L. Brahms section of his bookcase he'd deemed inappropriate for a woman her age. But if Imogen read them, then she would, too. She would take David's advice and start with the book he recommended. It would give her something to talk about with him when they next met.

The gentlemen made small talk and Abigail drew closer to Imogen. "Thank you for providing a distraction. I didn't know you read K.L. Brahms. You never mentioned reading the author before."

Imogen's smile was sincere. "I've read all sixteen editions."

"Sixteen?" Peter interrupted. "There are only fifteen published and it's been a good long while since the last. I was starting to think he'd given up writing."

"My mistake. It must be fifteen," Imogen assured him, but something in her manner did not seem truthful to Abigail's way of thinking. But with Peter now hovering and wanting to talk of this Brahms fellow again, she'd have to wait until they were alone to ask.

As Peter and Imogen discussed the books at length, Abigail eased away. They were really quite passionate about the stories in question and it was hard to understand the topic when she hadn't a clue as to the subject matter.

David left them to the discussion and drew closer to her. "I understand you've been calling on Mrs. Metcalf recently. That was very kind of you."

"Yes." Abigail met his gaze. "She was quite lost without her husband for a good number of weeks. His passing was peaceful. He was there for dinner and gone before breakfast, she said."

"Metcalf was entirely without fuss. It was one of the things I admired about him. I called on her today. She had her daughters and grandchildren visiting."

Abigail smiled. "Her family wishes her to move to Hove soon but she will not go. She says Brighton is the only place to be."

As she held David's gaze, a warmth invaded her chest. She was very fond of him. She might even have fallen in love. The realization made her want to throw her arms about him and never let him go again. But he was only here for a few days more. After that, she'd have to wait a year to see him again. That was simply too long. But how could she arrange any better? She bit her lip, thinking it over. Peter's situation cast a pall over all her plans. Would they even be living here when summer came round again? Would David feel inclined to visit her elsewhere once his business with Peter was done?

"Do you agree with her?" David's low pitched question caused her insides to jump.

"I do love Brighton."

But she didn't know if she could wait an entire year just for another chance to see David. Who knows, maybe when he was away in London he had a lady hoping to see him. She did not like the idea of losing him to another. And she certainly didn't want him kissing someone else.

"What's the matter?" he asked quietly.

"London is simply too far away from Brighton."

A look of agreement crossed his face. "I was thinking precisely the same thing, but it is not possible to move the great city based on only a wish."

"Then perhaps it is time to move the people." A movement at the doorway caught her eye, a sign that dinner was ready to be served. She winked at David, a very bold move to be certain given her brother stood several feet away and hurried to catch Imogen's arm.

As they gathered in the dining room, she hoped tonight's dinner would prove to David she was worthy of his notice. She wished with all her heart that he'd be so impressed by her skills as a hostess he would want her for his wife.

———— ◆ ————

"You are to be congratulated, Watson. Your sister has become an exemplary hostess," David said, meaning every word. He hadn't enjoyed a meal more in a very long time. Abigail had been warm and gracious, including him in the conversation when Imogen and Watson had returned to their contention over the wide appeal of K. L. Brahms' work. He could easily see Imogen found Watson's views amusing that some of the novels touched on the vulgar. As the author, she alone knew the source of her topics and why she'd chosen to write of them.

Despite his opinion that the works were inappropriate for very young ladies, Peter Watson appeared to be an avid fan. Watson could recall the precise order of publication and he could even quote certain passages that appealed to him.

"She enjoys entertaining." Watson pulled a bottle from a sideboard cupboard and filled two glasses. He passed one to David. "Not that we have done much of late."

David sipped, noting the flavor was not as agreeable as he was used to enjoying in the great city. However, Peter had given him the opening he needed to start their business discussion. He just needed to follow through. He set the glass down, but the words clogged in his throat. He swallowed, for the first time ever, utterly speechless when it came to discussing his client's finances. He had to do this. He coughed several times but nothing came to him as a way to start. In desperation, he returned to discussing Abigail. "I understand your sister had a successful visit to London," he said at last.

"Not so successful that she made a match, though she had a fair few interested. A pity. She really enjoyed her time in London. She was disappointed to return home when our month was up," Peter confided. He drained his glass and refilled it again.

It surprised him that Abigail had regretted leaving London when she'd been so dismissive of the gentlemen she'd met there. "I'm sure she was much admired," David agreed, resting back in the chair. "I was surprised some lucky fellow hadn't snapped her up."

"They'd have to catch her first." Peter shook his head. "My sister has very strong notions about marriage."

If she had dressed as she had tonight, wearing the sheerest of gowns with tiny capped sleeves, then the gentleman would have been clamoring all over themselves to reach her. She could have had any man she wanted. Keep his eyes from her low bodice had taken a toll on David's nerves during the meal. He'd imagined any number of ways to peel her out of the dress. "And what of you? We haven't really talked since my return. Have you set your heart on making a match yourself?"

Peter stared at him steadily. "That's unlikely."

"The right woman could do wonders for your circumstances," he said quietly. There, he'd done it. He'd introduced a subject that could lead to discussing Peter's finances and securing a bride with a fortune at the same time. Abigail should be pleased with him.

Peter sat forward in his chair suddenly. "I don't see a wife on your arm."

"My circumstances are different." He shrugged. "I've no need for a wife."

"You have the money to support one," Peter countered bitterly. "You're as rich as Croesus. You could have a wife and a mistress and not feel the pinch to your pocketbook."

"But I have little time for either."

"And I have ample time, but barely any money to support anyone but my sister." Peter loosened his cravat, face turning a deep shade of red at his confession. For a man normally full of jovial good spirits, the situation had severely curbed his lighter side.

David sighed. "I had hoped never to have this conversation with a friend. I wish our fathers had never started this. But you must understand what my partner demands I do while I am here. The debt cannot stand as it is. You must find a way out of this. A good marriage could considerably improve your life." Slowly, David removed the sealed letter from his pocket and slid it across the table.

Peter stared at it. "How long?"

"A month. I will return on the day to take possession of the house," David said quietly. He wouldn't let his partner come to Brighton. Knight would not be kind or patient as the Watsons took their leave.

Peter's shoulders sagged, his gaze dipping to the floor in defeat.

For the first time ever, David felt evil. He was robbing a

friend of his home. He'd become the antithesis of all he had hoped to be in his career. He wanted people to live a comfortable life. He simply couldn't do what he wanted for a man in Peter Watson's position.

As he reached for his wine glass to wash the sour taste from his mouth, Peter spoke. "Leave."

"Peter," David started.

But his friend's chin lifted. His eyes blazed with hate. "Take your money-grubbing ways out of my house. You are not to set foot within until month's end."

David sighed and stood. "As you wish."

He strode from the room and picked up his hat and gloves from the entrance table. A movement inside the parlor drew his eye. Abigail waited with Miss George by her side, her clenched hands and panicked expression the final sign he could no longer call himself a good man.

He knew this could happen but it hurt far more than he'd anticipated. Rather than speak to her, and risk Peter's temper, David backed toward the door and quickly let himself out. He should not have come to Brighton. He should have let Knight handle the matter himself and mourned the loss of friends at a distance.

Chapter Twelve

Glass shattered within the dining room. Abigail rushed there to see what Peter was about. She ducked as a wine bottle flew over her head to smash against the cream-papered walls. "Peter, what on earth is the matter with you?"

But the brother she knew and loved had fled. In his place was a caged beast, striding from one end of the small room to the other, hands waving about in agitation. She had never seen him this way before and he frightened her. He tore his hands through his hair, almost as if he meant to rip it from his head, but he didn't stop moving.

Determined to end the madness, Abigail stepped into his path. "Peter, stop a moment and tell me what's wrong." She grabbed for him, but he eluded her. He backed away quickly, and then spun for the door. Unfortunately, Imogen stood between him and the door and, in his haste, Peter didn't see her. He crashed into Imogen and she was knocked to the hard floor, a startled *oomph* leaving her lips.

Abigail hurried across the room as Peter lifted Imogen to her feet, apologies tumbling from his lips so rapidly Imogen had no chance to respond. All of a sudden, Imogen captured his face between her hands and held him still. "Accidents happen, Mr. Watson. I'm uninjured."

Abigail's brother closed his eyes briefly as Imogen moved her fingers over his red cheeks, and then he wrenched himself away, rushing for the door and leaving without even taking his hat or gloves.

"Peter, wait," Abigail called after him, but he never replied. She rushed to the front steps and peered down Cavendish Place. The street was deserted at this hour and after a time she had no choice but to shut the front door. He would come back soon. He and David must have quarreled, although she hadn't heard a word of their conversation from the parlor.

He would calm down soon enough. He simply needed time to take it all in. She followed Imogen into the parlor, and then realized her friend was limping. "Imogen, you *are* hurt."

"So it would seem. I landed somewhat awkwardly. I'll be all right in a little while."

Imogen sat on the couch, but it was clear from the way she winced that her injury resided on her bottom. "Where will he go, do you think?"

Abigail rubbed her temple hard. "I hate to speculate, but I hope he does not go to another hell. That won't solve the problem."

"No. Gambling now will not solve anything, but could get you deeper into trouble. I wish he would come back soon. I do not like to think of you here alone if he returns in a temper."

"Peter is not a violent person. I am sure today is an aberration." Abigail nibbled at her fingertip, uncertain of what to do next. It wasn't like Peter to rush off into the night without a word to where he was going. Should she follow him?

Imogen pursed her lips. "Troubled times calls for family and friends to stick together not bottle everything up inside. Did he confide in anyone?"

"Not that I ever learned. He never really told me of his financial issues, remember."

They both jumped as three knocks rattled the front door.

"Simpson will see who it is." Abigail peered at Imogen as she gingerly repositioned herself on the couch. "Are you sure there is nothing I can do for you?"

Imogen shook her head. "It's mostly my pride that is bruised."

Simpson's slow steps echoed in the hall and then male voices sounded. At last, Simpson came to the parlor doorway. "Mr. Hawke wishes to inquire if you are in need, Miss Watson. He is quite concerned."

Abigail's heart raced. If she asked David to find Peter and bring him home again, would he be willing? "Please ask him to come in, Mr. Simpson, so I may reassure him in person."

"I did ask him to step inside, but he has refused." Simpson glanced over his shoulder before he spoke. "I believe the master did banish Mr. Hawke from entering the house ever again before he stormed out."

Abigail jumped to her feet. Why would Peter be so cruel to their friend? It wasn't David's fault Peter was in debt. She rushed for the front door. David waited on the pavement, pacing to and fro.

When he saw her, his shoulders sagged. "I shouldn't be here, but I had to check. Is everything all right within?"

"Yes, everything is fine." She glanced up and down the street and saw more than one head at the curtains, outlined by the candlelight behind them. "Please come in."

"I am afraid I may not. I wanted to see for myself that you remain unharmed." David stepped closer to the door. "I heard glass break."

His voice dipped to a rough murmur and Abigail's stomach tumbled all over itself. She wanted to throw herself into his arms, but with the residents of the street watching them, she didn't dare. "It was nothing. Peter was upset tonight. I'm quick on my feet."

A soft smile tugged at David's mouth. "I do recall that. Forgive me for intruding. I saw him rush off and couldn't help myself."

He skimmed his fingertips along her cheek in a fleeting caress.

"Mr. Hawke," Imogen called, limping toward the door and breaking the spell between them. "May I have a word in private?"

Her hard glance caused a blush to heat Abigail's cheek. She should not allow David to touch her so tenderly where anyone passing by could see. Yet she couldn't seem to find her good sense around him.

David nodded as Imogen joined them at the door. "Of

course."

Imogen kissed her cheek. "Try not to worry. I will see you soon."

"You're going?"

Her friend nodded. "I shall gather Walter and set out on Peter's trail to ensure he does nothing foolish." She stepped out onto the street, whispered something to David that Abigail could not hear and moved away. After a few steps, David glanced over his shoulder, but the expression on his face was as bleak as the day of his arrival.

------------◆------------

"If you toy with my friends affections for sport I shall be very cross with you Mr. Hawke. I shall name a terrible villain after you and plot a grisly demise."

David gulped, very sure Miss George would paint him the worst bounder. "I hardly know how to answer you. I'd not planned any of this."

For a man who planned everything he was completely out of his depth when it came to his pretty neighbor. He needed to take greater care to hide his interest.

"Then I suggest you start planning how it will end. I hope not badly for Abigail. She has always looked up to you. Ah, here we are."

"Miss George, might I inquire as to your plan?" David looked down at the woman on his arm. "Rushing after Peter Watson might not be advisable given his mood."

"I do not believe allowing him to wallow in his current frame of mind would be wise." She rapped on her front door, smiled at her housekeeper. "Would you know the location of my brother, Mrs. Perkins?"

"He's at supper, miss."

"Ah, perfect. If he's already eaten then he'll be an amiable companion for a stroll. If any woman wanted to snare my brother for a wife all they need do is see his meals were delivered promptly. Thank you for your time this evening, Mr. Hawke."

She curtsied to him and then quickly shut the door. David remained where he stood, trying to figure out what Miss George thought she could achieve by chasing after Peter in the middle of the night. Did every woman in Cavendish Place have no care for her reputation?

David raked his fingers through his hair, speculating on the increase of grey appearing at his temples. "Not my problem," he muttered to himself. There really was nothing more he could do.

He slowly retraced his steps, glancing at the façade of the Watson's residence to see if Abigail lingered at a window. The curtain didn't move and with a pang of disappointment he went to his own door and let himself inside.

His townhouse was silent, save for the whimpers emanating from the rear of the house. He hurried to the kitchen and scooped the puppy up against his chest. "Here I am, Princess. No need to fret."

The animal licked his fingers and wagged its tail so much David feared it would do itself an injury. After soothing the beast, David stepped out into the dark rear yard. He set the puppy down in a small patch of grass and looked up into the night sky.

Even with the puppy for company, he was lonely.

Perhaps he *should* consider finding a wife.

But the only woman he could imagine spending his nights and days with was Abigail and now he couldn't even call on her to court her properly. Peter would never agree, given the business between them. The thought of how long it might take to repair their friendship wasn't comforting. He could be waiting a long time and he didn't want to wait another day.

He glanced at the rear of Abigail's house, where he knew her bedchamber to be. It was dark which must mean she had already turned in for the night. Disappointment filled him. He was alone again and he was tired of it.

He sat down on a patch of grass and considered what to do. Should he approach Peter first or try to get Abigail alone again to see if she was interested? She'd clearly stated she wasn't looking for a husband. Would she accept if he asked her?

The rear garden gate creaked and he looked up. Abigail

approached slowly, her head tilted to one side, still wearing the dress that had tortured him during dinner. "I was afraid you had company for a moment."

He patted the pup who had just taken an interest in the tip of his boot. "Miss Watson, may I introduce Princess? Princess, you have the honor of meeting our remarkable young neighbor."

Abigail knelt beside him and stretched her fingers out to the pup. When Princess licked at her fingers a happy smile flittered over her face. Abigail had a tender heart and made friends very easily. He would like to see her smile so every day. He was sure the effort to make her happy would be worth any sacrifice.

He yearned to pull her into his arms and promise everything would turn out for the best. "I take it Peter has not returned."

Her head lowered and her fingers clasped together. "No."

"Abigail, may I ask you a question?"

Her smile was immediate. "Of course."

"Why are you here?"

She shrugged and returned her attention to Princess. "I feel comfortable with you."

"Is that all?"

She picked up the puppy and cuddled it against her chest. "You leave soon."

"True." And he'd never been so reluctant to return to the capital before.

She peeked at him from beneath her lashes. "It'll be another year before I can talk to you again."

He nodded, his heartbeat increasing at the idea she might miss him when he was in London. He eased closer until they sat side by side in the dark. "I must return to the city. I have responsibilities."

"I know and do admire you for that. But, it becomes very quiet when you are gone. I don't want to miss a moment."

David's thoughts tumbled over themselves. He, too, would miss her and treasured these stolen moments, more than he ever realized he would. David didn't want them to end when he left. He wanted Abigail in his life. He stood and held out his hand. "Princess should be put to bed."

Abigail laid her hand in his and allowed him to raise her to her feet. "She's lovely. Where did she come from?"

He stood aside so she could enter his home first and quietly shut then locked the door behind them. They were alone; the first time he had willingly, intentionally, done something that might ruin her reputation. And he did not care. "I found her under a cabbage actually."

"Really. I thought that sort of thing was simply for fairytales and little children's bedtime stories."

Abigail's laughter filled his house, causing him to join in. "Hence my decision to name her Princess. Do you like her?"

"I do. She has a sweet disposition."

"I wondered if you might take her."

Her gaze rose to his. "I would love to, except I have no idea where I'll be living soon."

He took the pup and settled the animal back in her bed. "I've been giving that some thought tonight and I had considered offering Peter my house to live in until he could make other arrangements."

Abigail backed from the room, one eye on the drowsy puppy. "He wouldn't accept."

David followed and joined her in the hall. Princess whimpered and then fell silent. He hoped she would be a deep sleeper tonight. "Then my offer would be to you. I know how much you love Brighton. It distresses me that I'll be responsible for forcing you away."

She pressed a finger to his lips, ending the string of apologies crowding his mind. "I'll be fine, David. I'm not completely helpless."

This business was in no way fair to her. "Even so."

She drew closer, rose up on her toes, and brushed her lips against his in a fleeting kiss. "Shh, don't worry about me so much."

David searched her face, saw nothing but affection and trust there. He swallowed. He simply couldn't walk away from Abigail when her future was so uncertain. "I don't seem able to prevent that."

She grinned. "Then you don't really mind me being here."

David lifted a hand to her cheek and stroked his thumb over

the soft surface. No other woman had ever gotten under his skin like this. He could not, would not, fight the instinct to keep her close. To do everything he could to protect her and keep her for himself was imperative. There was only Abigail. "No. In fact, I think it would be best for you to stay."

When she nodded, David scooped her into his arms and carried her upstairs to his bedchamber before she thought better of her decision.

Chapter Thirteen

Days of frustration fell away as David closed his bedchamber door behind them. Abigail had a look in her eye David liked very much. A look that said she agreed with his decision to make love to her tonight. He couldn't deny his feelings for her if he wanted to, and he did not fight the joy this moment brought him. He slowly lowered her to her feet but kept her close as a bubble of happiness crowded his chest. "Abigail, you shouldn't be here now, not yet anyway, but I won't deny I want you more than I can say."

"I'm exactly where I want to be," she assured him. Abigail smiled shyly at him and he fell completely, irrevocably, in love with her as she kicked off her shoes.

He dipped his head, and skimmed his lips across hers.

Days between kisses faded. He was back in that moment when he knew he was doing wrong but was utterly powerless to stop. He should wait until they were married or at the very least wait until the marriage contract had been signed. But she touched his chest lightly and such a small sensation wasn't enough. He pulled her firmly against his body and held her closer.

She said nothing to discourage him, but she encircled his neck with her arms and tangled her fingers into his hair at the nape. Goose flesh swept his body. David plundered her mouth, drinking in her taste, her warmth and her sweet response to his kisses.

When he drew back, she had closed her eyes. "Abigail," he whispered.

Her lashes fluttered as she looked up at him. "David."

He kissed her cheek, her neck, and across her collarbone. "I am afraid, as much as I admire how pretty you are this evening, I'm going to delight in mussing you up."

Abigail tightened her grip about his neck and smiled up at him with bright trusting eyes. "I think I would like that. Tell me what to do?"

David sucked in a breath and ran his hands over her back. "Simply being here is enough. How could I be so fortunate as to win you?"

Abigail molded herself to him, her hands restless in his hair. David kissed her again with all the pent-up passion a week of wanting—and fighting that want—could provide. Tomorrow he would buy Abigail a pretty ring to place on her finger, speak to Peter to make their union official. She would never lack any comfort, but tonight he would make Abigail his forever.

He plunged his tongue into her mouth, tasting, teasing enough to make Abigail moan. He drew back to look at her. Her skin was flushed, lips parted and damp. He kissed her softly and then her eyes snapped opened again, shrewdly assessing him. "Has anyone ever told you that you're wonderful?"

"No. But I'm sure I'm only that way because of you."

Her hands fluttered over his chest and finally settled at the top of his waistcoat. She undid the first button and bit her lip. She moved her fingers down to the next and the next until his waistcoat hung open.

David lifted his hands to her beautiful hair and carefully removed the pins. The pale strands tumbled down her back in waves and he tossed the pins over his shoulder as impatience seized him. He ran his fingers through the strands. "This is the second time I've seen your hair down."

Abigail pushed his coat and waistcoat from his shoulders and they fell to the floor in a messy heap. A frown marred her brow. "When was the first?"

"You were seven, I think, and tangled in a tree. Your hair has grown since then."

A small laugh left her lips. "All of me has grown since then."

"I noticed." He kissed the tip of her nose, rather humbled that he would be her first and last lover. He would make sure she never regretted her choice. "You take my breath away with your beauty."

Abigail rose on her toes and caught his mouth with hers. David cupped her head, secured his fingers in her hair and surrendered to his fate—Abigail.

She caught his shirt and pulled the material free of his trousers. Her hands slid over his skin and he sucked in a shocked gasp. His body strained for more.

David fumbled for the fastenings of her gown but their location defeated him. "I'm all thumbs," he said in apology.

A smile flittered across Abigail's face as she stepped back. "Here. It opens this way."

She pulled a cord at the neck and thanks to the little sleeves, the gown loosened enough to slide to her hips without a struggle. She wriggled a bit and the fabric fell to her feet. David's pulse raced. She stood in just her chemise, her small breasts peaked and visible through the thin garment.

He caught her hand in his and raised it to his lips. "I am unworthy of such a gift, but I would be an utter fool not to accept."

He kissed the back of her hand, and then her palm. Slowly, he drew his lips up the length of her arm until she was once more standing in his embrace. Her breasts brushed his chest with each unsteady breath she took.

"Do people make love standing up? If so, I'm not sure my limbs will hold me."

David swept her into his arms again and carried her to his bed. He lowered her gently to the mattress and stood back. So lovely. He kicked off his footwear before he followed. "Not always. You need never do anything you don't want. This can be enough."

"It's not enough," she whispered unsteadily. "It couldn't possibly be."

She brought herself against him, rubbing like a cat and kissing him until he lost all reason. Her chemise disappeared quickly, as did his shirt and breeches. When they were both naked and panting, David drew her under him and kissed her nose. "I never imagined this when I came home, but I doubt I will ever forget this summer."

He smoothed a hand down her side and along her thigh before hooking her leg around his thigh. Abigail shifted, opening herself to him and tightened her hold. "No more talk."

She rose to kiss him again and teased him with her tongue. He groaned and shifted his hips until he brushed her curls with his erection. He drew back. "I'm told this, making love the first time, may not be pleasant for you."

She cupped his face. "Nothing you could do would ever disappoint me."

David pushed against her, discovering her body was closed to him. He rocked his hips, prepared to take things as slow as she needed to avoid injuring her more than necessary. Wet warmth claimed him as he inched further inside. He slowed his advance and kissed her lips. Abigail panted but her expression showed no pain.

He smoothed the hair from her cheek, and then lifted his weight from her body. The movement drove him deeper and a quick flicker of pain crossed her face. He stopped until she relaxed. Then moved again, claiming her as gently as he could.

When he reached her limit, he fell to one arm and kissed her mouth. "Are you all right, my love?"

Her breath came in little pants, drawing his attention to her untouched breasts. "Is there more?"

He slowly covered the perfect mound and stroked his thumb over the hard peak until she gasped. There were any number of sensual pleasures a devoted and thorough man could share with his wife. David would delight in each and every moment. "So much more, I promise you."

He drew back and thrust in, watching Abigail for signs of pain. His slow approach had worked well, for after a time she clung to him, fingers digging into his back and moaning softly to each thrust. David had never felt so alive before. So connected to another person. Making love to Abigail was more fulfilling than he'd ever dreamed. He slowed his thrusts and deepened them, aiming to bring her greater pleasure.

Abigail's eyes widened as he filled her. Her head tipped back and she pressed her lips together. He brought his mouth beside her ear and nibbled at her throat. "Tell me. Don't hold back."

She gasped and clutched at him. "I don't know what to say."

"Do you want me to stop?" Given the way she held onto him, he thought he knew the answer.

"Don't stop. Don't. Don't. Never. Never. Never stop." More words tumbled from her lips. Words pleading for something she couldn't name. David held her tightly to him, giving up his own needs altogether in order to provide Abigail with sensations she required most. Her fingers bit deeper into his skin, her thighs tightened around his hips and a wail suddenly left her mouth.

He held himself still as she shuddered, drinking in the pleasure of her first release. However, he couldn't remain so for long and he quickly succumbed to desire, whispering her name against her throat as he climaxed. When she relaxed, he withdrew, still hard, still desiring more but afraid he was crushing her.

He eased onto his side, drew Abigail against his chest, and plotted out their new future. In the morning he would write to his partner at the bank, explain why he wouldn't return as planned and ask him to call in a few favors: namely the purchase of a special license to marry as quickly as possible and to organize the lease of a larger and far nicer apartment. Knight had excellent taste and good connections. He could have it all arranged, and David would move in, before Abigail even arrived in the capital. Once his letter was on its way, he would meet with Peter Watson and ask for Abigail's hand in marriage.

Abigail pressed her lips to his chest. "David."

"Yes, my love."

"Hmm," she murmured sleepily as she cuddled against him. "I like the way you say that."

"Good, because I intend to use the endearment often." He ran a hand down her spine, over her hip and along her leg as far as he could reach. Her skin was silky soft, and so very tempting. She snuggled closer to him, pressing against his erection that hadn't softened very much.

She stroked her hands over his shoulders, fingers brushing over his skin possessively, and swept down his sides. "Are you all right?"

"That is the question I should be asking you." David laughed softly. "But I've never felt better in my life, Abigail. I hope you feel the same. Thank you for seducing me."

She sat up suddenly, hair tangled and free across her breasts. "Did I do that? Really?"

He smiled and lay back with an arm behind his head. "I believe you did."

Her eyebrows rose as if she found the idea ridiculous and then she climbed on top of him, thighs holding him in place beneath her slight weight, soft hands pressed to his chest, hips perilously close to his lingering erection. "I would never have believed I could before tonight," she murmured.

He pushed her hair aside to expand his splendid view of her body. "You seduce me with every breath you take."

He brushed a thumb over a nipple until it hardened to a tight peak. When Abigail took her bottom lip between her teeth, he brushed over it again. Her lips curled into a broad smile and she leaned down to kiss him. Powerless to resist, David kissed her in return and then showed her there was more than one way to make love.

Chapter Fourteen

———◆———

Abigail suffered Imogen's embrace in a state of utter shock as her friend whispered in her ear, "Now we *will* be sisters. No matter what happens we will always have each other."

She drew away slowly. She'd only caught a few hours rest last night and her mind was a little fuzzy still. "Excuse me, but did you just say you were to be married?"

Imogen's smile dimmed. "Yes, that is exactly what I said."

Abigail squeezed her eyes shut and opened them again. She sat in her brother's parlor, taking tea with her best friend and for a change her brother appeared attentive. She must be dreaming this nightmare. "To each other?"

"Well, of course to each other," her brother bit out.

So she *had* heard correctly. Her brother and best friend were to be married at the end of the month. Yet Abigail couldn't fathom how a union between them could possibly work. They barely spoke, and Peter always left the house when Imogen came to pay a social call. They were not marrying for love.

Imogen's smile brightened suddenly. "Are you not happy for us, Abigail?"

She quickly caught her friend's hands, noting the cold clamminess of her fingers and the fervent return grip. Perhaps Imogen wasn't as confident about getting married to Peter as she had first appeared to be. Had she been tricked into it?

Since her brother hovered at Imogen's side, she couldn't ask her question right now. But later, she would get to the bottom of what Peter had done. She would support Imogen's decision to call off the union if she had been forced to act against her better judgment.

"Of course I am." She forced a smile and made an effort to act normally. "It's just so unexpected and sudden. I had no idea my brother was so enamored of you he would bring himself to the point. I hope you were suitably romantic, Peter. Imogen deserves the very best."

Imogen's gaze dipped to their joined hands and she drew away.

"Sometimes a swift decision about these matters is for the best," Peter mumbled, throwing a quick glance behind him as if looking for someone. "Would you excuse me for a moment?"

When he was gone, Abigail peered into Imogen's face. "Tell me exactly how he came to propose. Quickly, before he returns."

Imogen sighed. "Another time. I must be going. I have an appointment with Mr. Hawke shortly. I simply wanted you to know everything will come good now. You'll never have to leave Brighton or this house. You have my word everything will be well again."

Imogen gave her one last long hug and then hurried out, without lingering to say farewell to Peter. A vast silence stretched in her wake. This was not a love match. Not even close. The stiff formality between Imogen and Peter left her in no doubt they were ill suited to be in each other's pockets for the rest of her life. How soon would they regret their hasty decision?

Abigail knew exactly what love felt like. She was certainly in love with David and had hardly been able to tear herself away from his bed in the early hours of the morning. She had no regrets about giving herself to him. He cared for her and in time, perhaps, he would come to love her just as strongly as she did him. If he proposed, she would happily move to London.

But her first concern now had to be extracting her friend from this farcical arrangement. Imogen would not be happy as Peter's wife.

She turned and went in search of her brother. Peter stood in the dining room, appearing deep in thought as he stared out at the garden.

When he didn't acknowledge her presence, Abigail cleared her throat to get his attention. "What have you done?"

His brow creased as he turned around. "I've done what's best for you."

"Best for me?" Abigail's blood boiled. "What about what is best for her? How can marrying my best friend be in any way good? You're not in love. Don't deny it."

"You place too much value on love," he mumbled. "This arrangement will save us."

"Arrangement! And who will save Imogen from you? She deserves to marry someone who will look after her, not a man who doesn't appreciate her sacrifice," she bit out savagely.

Peter's skin paled and Abigail moved closer, hands clenched. "If you cause her misery I swear I will make you wish you had not. She deserves better. You both do."

His shoulders slumped. "I know I don't deserve her. But she made a very good argument for a marriage between us. I swear I will do everything in my power to ensure she never regrets her offer."

Abigail gaped. "Imogen made the offer of marriage?"

He nodded. "I take it she didn't mention this was her idea in the first place?"

Abigail pressed her hands to her face. It wasn't Imogen's idea at all, it was hers. This was Abigail's fault for confiding so much to Imogen about their situation. She may not have asked outright, but she'd likely influenced Imogen's decision to offer herself and her inheritance so she and Peter could stay in Brighton. Once the words were spoken Peter and Imogen would be trapped.

What had she done?

After a time, her brother excused himself and left her alone in the parlor. Glass clicked against glass in the connecting room and she thought over the events of last evening. She should not have let Imogen pursue Peter into the night. She should at least have accompanied her to ensure she didn't do such a foolish thing.

But at the time Imogen must have been throwing her future away, Abigail had been in David's arms.

She shuddered. A loveless marriage. It was what she had planned for Peter, after all. She just hadn't expected Imogen to be the one to sacrifice herself to keep a roof over their heads. She hadn't even known Imogen had such a grand fortune to temp her brother into accepting such an arrangement in the first place. She'd assumed all her talk of investments was merely for a trifling sum. If Imogen were indeed an heiress then perhaps David, as her banker, could advise her to call it off. Peter wasn't exactly a good investment.

How sad she'd cautioned Imogen against him, yet attempted to lure Melanie Merton to be his bride. Peter spent all his time carousing, hiding from his responsibilities. How could Imogen chain herself to such a man?

She covered her face with her hands and rocked forward.

"There is a delivery for you," Peter said from the doorway.

Abigail darted a quick look at her brother. He held a bouquet of flowers in his hand. "They're pretty," she said.

His brow creased as he came forward. "There's no note so it seems you have a secret admirer. Any ideas who might have sent them?"

"No," Abigail lied. Her hands trembled as she took them. "Thank you."

Peter cleared his throat. "I'm going out for some air first, but Imogen insists I meet with Hawke today and end the disagreement between us. I wouldn't bother but he's to draw up the marriage contract—Imogen insists—before he returns to London and then we can put him from our minds for another year. I'll see you later, possibly not until dinner."

Abigail nodded and glanced down at the bouquet in her hands, her heart aching with sadness. Last night David had said he worried about her. That he couldn't seem to stop. Had he sent the flowers to show her he was thinking of her now, or was this his way of saying goodbye?

Although his concern had been sincere, he had not made her any promises beyond last night. He had claimed she'd seduced him and had reminded her he was leaving. At the time, she had not wanted to dwell on how she would feel later. But now the remembrance of his words caused her eyes to fill with tears and she blinked them back swiftly. He would leave in a few days and then she would have to wait a whole year to be in his arms again. Although new to love, Abigail wasn't sure how she would stand the separation.

Chapter Fifteen

David had penned a long letter to his business partner in London and sent it off well before the appointed time to meet with Walter and Imogen George. Truth be told, he'd been awake for hours. He'd bolted out of bed the minute he'd realized Abigail had left his side. Despite rushing downstairs in a state of shocking undress, Abigail had already vanished into the Brighton early morning.

He was surprised but not alarmed by her departure. With each encounter, they ran the risk she could be seen and face social ruin for their antics. Marriage to him, and a swift one, would be best in this situation.

He grinned, pleased with the way his life was headed. It was ridiculous how happy he felt, but he could not help himself. He'd requested his mother's old bedchamber aired and cleaned, fresh sheets placed on the bed, not that he had any intention of letting Abigail sleep alone. When he'd spied the flower seller on his way back from an early morning swim with Valentine, he'd doubled back and paid the old woman handsomely to deliver a bunch to Abigail. It was a pity he couldn't have penned a note to go with them. For now he would have to be patient, at least until he'd secured Peter's agreement to let them marry.

A knock sounded on the door and he bounded down the hall to let the George's in with an eager wave of his hand. "Good morning, George."

"Hawke," Walter George tumbled across his threshold without meeting his gaze.

David frowned, glancing at Imogen following behind, only then noticing her hand secured firmly around Peter Watson's arm. "Miss George. Good morning. Mr. Watson. What a pleasant surprise."

They passed him with a cool nod and he closed the door behind them. Although puzzled by the silent trio, he quickly turned his mind to the task at hand. "I was unaware Mr. Watson would be joining us. Do make yourselves at home in the study while I gather up another chair."

"Thank you," Miss George murmured.

David hurried down the hall, spoke to his housekeeper to request an extra setting to the tea tray, and then returned to the front of the house with a chair for Peter Watson. He sat behind his desk and looked at those before him.

Walter leaned forward. "Me first this time, and then I'll leave you three to discuss matters."

David extracted the carefully prepared report on Walter's investments and account and handed it over. Walter gave the page the briefest of glances and then folded it. "Even better results than last year. Thank you." He stood, held out his hand to David. "Swimming tomorrow?"

David shook it. "Absolutely."

"I'll see myself out." When Walter shuffled past Imogen and Peter, his expression changed. He frowned at his sister and Peter Watson, shook his head, and then shrugged away whatever concerned him.

The front door closed with a hollow thud just as the mantle clock chimed eleven. "I. Ah. Wasn't expecting to see you here, Mr. Watson. I trust everything is well at home?"

Watson nodded, his gaze sliding to Imogen.

She held herself rigidly. "Mr. Hawke, I have always been very impressed with your discretion concerning my business affairs. I am in need of your services once again."

"Oh, in what way may I help you?" He reached for paper and ink, ready to jot notes down should the need arise.

"I should like a marriage contract drawn up."

David sucked in a sharp breath and looked up again. "Marriage? Yours? To whom?"

She cut her gaze to Peter.

David stole a glance at Peter Watson. The poor man had his hands clenched on his thighs in a very agitated fashion. David stilled. *Imogen had been on Peter Watson's arm.* What had the desperate man done last night to bring this surprise announcement about? He put the pen down and pushed up his sleeves. "Would you care to share with me the events of last night?" He rolled his shoulders and stood.

"Oh, goodness, look at you." Imogen laughed, brittle and higher pitched than her usual tone. "Sit down, Mr. Hawke. This situation is entirely of my own making and there is absolutely no need for you to be concerned."

"I wondered why Walter appeared in a hurry to leave us this morning. He usually stays a good bit longer. I take it he doesn't approve of this decision," David said, casting an accusing glance at Peter Watson.

For his part, Peter appeared highly embarrassed. He refused to meet David's eye. "He'll come around eventually," he mumbled.

"What my brother thinks is not for discussion. This *is* what I want."

David listened to Imogen's surprisingly steady voice with growing concern. He had written several documents for clients before, so he knew exactly what the contract should entail and none of her requests were challenged by Peter. But the things left out of the conversation troubled him.

"I'll make copies after you've gone and will deliver them to your home as soon as possible." He glanced at Miss George. "Valentine Radley can keep a secret, Miss George. He would make a good witness if you are agreeable."

She nodded slowly. "I suppose the secret cannot remain so forever."

"What secret?" Peter Watson asked, glancing between them.

David caught Imogen's eye and saw the plea in her expression. She didn't know how to tell him. She'd kept the secret so close for so long she appeared to be without words. How would K.L. Brahms' greatest admirer take the news that the author was the woman whom he would marry?

He picked up his papers and shuffled them until they were neat. "As you may be aware, I have been privy to Miss George's business dealings for some years. As her banker, I have intimate knowledge of the source of her funds."

Peter nodded. "Of course. Her aunt left her money some years ago."

David shook his head. "That isn't true. We at the bank have worked very hard to keep the real source of her wealth, and the fact that Miss George is in fact an heiress, a secret from society and her friends. I trust you, too, will act with the utmost discretion. After all, if word got out after you were married you might find yourselves in an uncomfortable position socially."

Peter glanced around the room, panic clear on his face. "What's going on?"

"Mr. Watson." David gestured to Miss George. "I have the honor of introducing you to K. L. Brahms."

Peter's eyes widened. He looked at Miss George, at David, and then back to Miss George again—his expression one of utter disbelief. "You cannot be serious."

"I am indeed serious," David assured him. "You know me. I would never lie about such an important matter. Miss George is the author of the works you admired so much the other evening."

Miss George met David's gaze and shrugged. "I knew it was too much to hope for. Thank you for your time, Mr. Hawke. I should like to speak with you about another matter when you deliver the papers."

He stood. "Anything for you."

Miss George stood. She swept her gaze over the man still seated at her side, and then quit the room. David followed to see her out and when he came back, Peter still stared at the spot she'd been sitting.

David spread Miss George's papers before him, ready for the moment when he could finish his work. He glanced at his companion. The frown marring Peter Watson's brow had grown.

"You were pulling my leg, Hawke, weren't you?"

"I never joke where a client is involved. If you want any further particulars concerning K.L. Brahms then you will need to speak to her."

"Those books are," he said before swallowing and loosening his cravat as if it were strangling him. "Dear God. How long have you known?"

David smiled tightly. "Years. I remember the conversation being as startling as it appears to be to you. She is a talented writer. So much wit and energy in her work."

"Brahms is a man. Everyone thinks that." Peter covered his head. "She must have found my dinner conversation utterly ridiculous. Who else knows?"

David shrugged. "Her editor in London, of course. That is all I am aware of."

Peter wiped his hand over his face. "Do you think Abigail has known all along? They are as close as sisters and I cannot believe they have any secrets left to share. Those books are scandalous."

"Hardly that." David sat forward. "Miss George shows the world as it is. If anything, her female readers can learn something from her cautionary tales. But Miss George has never indicated she has told Abigail her secret. At dinner last night, I thought your sister appeared unaware of the contents of the books."

"Thank God she does not know. I'll have to put a stop to this. There will be no more of that nonsense."

"Why would you do that? K.L. Brahms is saving you from ruin and future publications will keep you on solid ground financially. Last night you were impassioned on the subject. What harm can come of letting her continue as she has?"

"The revelation will damage my sister's chances of making a good match one day," Watson countered. He stood suddenly. "I need to think."

"Watson, before you go I have to ask; may I call upon your sister today?"

Watson nodded. "Yes. Yes. Forgive me. I never should have behaved so boorishly." He hurried out and when he was gone David leaned back in his chair, quite certain Peter Watson had no inkling of the type of call David wanted to make. However, he was too wise to set Watson straight.

Chapter Sixteen

"I cannot believe you would do this," Abigail argued. "You don't even care for him. You said you would only marry if there was love involved."

A sad smile crossed Imogen's face and deepened Abigail's distress. "I know. But a woman has the right to change her mind. Your brother is a decent sort and I can help. Would you really rather have Miss Radley and her scowls than me for a sister?"

"No. Of course not. I only want what's best for you."

Imogen patted her hand. "This will be. I'm sure your brother and I will rub along well. After all, he'll have what he wants and likely go his own way. Marriage will give me quite a bit of freedom. We'll not need to wait and arrange a suitable chaperone to accompany us when we go out anymore. It will be my pleasure to take you anywhere you want to go."

Abigail nibbled on a fingertip. A week ago the idea would have appealed to her. But not like this.

"We could go to London on occasion," Imogen offered. "You enjoyed your time there."

"I did but, I doubt your time will be entirely your own."

"Why wouldn't it be?" Imogen stood and moved to the window.

"Well, you will be Peter's wife and he will wish to spend time with you. He may not like you leaving Brighton without him."

Abigail stared at Imogen's back, saw her shoulders rise at the idea of being followed around by her brother. If Abigail were to marry David, she'd be ecstatic to spend her days in his company. Not to mention the nights. It did not seem likely Imogen experienced the same sense of anticipation about becoming Peter's constant companion.

"Your brother was in my company this morning when I saw Mr. Hawke. I believe the air has been cleared between them although they may never return to their former footing."

A blush burned Abigail's skin. "He leaves soon." Her voice sounded so small and pathetic to even her own ears that she buried her face in her hands to hide her distress. The deadline for David's departure was approaching too rapidly for her comfort.

Imogen faced her and smoothed her hair back from her face gently. "What am I going to do with you? Do you really want him?"

Abigail slowly nodded. She'd thought of him every other moment. She wanted to know what he did with his day, all alone in his empty house. She didn't like him being on his own. He should have someone with him to make him laugh.

"Your brother promised me he would end his foolish plan to banish Hawke from visiting. Absurd idea. I imagine if Hawke's heart is engaged and he's the good man you claim, following that discussion he might request to call on you."

Abigail surged to her feet, anxious she might have missed him. "Why didn't you say so earlier?"

Imogen chuckled. "Well, you've been berating me so well for settling on a marriage of convenience I thought you'd best get it out of your system as soon as possible." Imogen kissed her cheek. "Go on. Off with you. You'll never be satisfied until you see Hawke again."

Abigail hugged her friend tightly to her. "Thank you." She fled for home, snatching up her bonnet and gloves from the startled housekeeper's hands. She burst onto the street, turned for her house and barreled into a broad chest.

"Miss Watson," David murmured as he steadied her. "What a pleasant surprise."

Abigail stared up into David's face and couldn't contain her smile. "Good morning."

He winked. "I had just called on you, but was told you were out visiting your friend. May I walk you home?"

When he held out his arm, Abigail blushed as she took it. "Thank you."

They strolled the very short distance to her house and when she entered, David followed her inside and handed his hat and gloves to her butler. "I trust everything is in order."

Abigail stepped into the parlor, conscious that the man who'd introduced her to the delights of the bedroom lingered a painfully short distance away and she couldn't touch him yet. She glanced around him and caught her butler's eye. "Simpson, might we have tea sent up and make sure to include the seed cake that was made this morning."

"My favorite," David murmured when Simpson had gone, leaving the door ajar.

Abigail grinned and sat down on the settee. David sat at her side, turned slightly so he faced her. He held her gaze a long moment and then he swooped in to kiss her lips. When he lifted his head, Abigail's senses were spinning wildly.

"I missed you," he whispered.

The heat in his eyes drew her closer to him. At the last second, Abigail found the sense not to throw herself into his arms. Simpson would return at any moment. She shook her head to clear it. "That's what every woman wants to hear."

"Hmm." David caressed her cheek. "Is all well between Imogen and yourself? I fear the proposal has caught you unawares since I was sure you had your sights set on an entirely different bride for Peter."

She caught his hand and held it tightly against her skin. "Yes, I'm just worried she'll come to regret her decision. She doesn't love him and he surely does not love her."

"I thought that the case, too. But everything has been arranged now and there is nothing to stop them. The banns will be called on Sunday and the marriage should happen shortly thereafter. You'll be glad to know the bank has no further interest in this house."

"So you're free to return to London." Abigail stood and

hurried to the front window, staring outside at the bright sunny day without really seeing anything beautiful in it. He was leaving and there wasn't anything she could do to change his mind. He had responsibilities and he would honor them. Tears threatened to fall down her cheek and she held them back ruthlessly. When he was gone, she would blubber all she liked. But she wouldn't waste what was left of their time together.

"I'm not as free as you think. I made a promise to stay, if you remember. But there is one other important affair that must be settled before I could possibly return to the capital. Something that has become very, very urgent and important to me."

"Princess." She sagged. "I suppose now my brother's future is assured I am able to take care of her for you."

"Good." He moved to stand behind her, hands resting lightly on her upper arms. "However, she is not at the forefront of my mind right now. And if I can resolve that issue to my satisfaction then Princess' care will be assured."

Puzzled, Abigail faced him. His expression had become serious once more. "What is it?"

"I need you to do something for me," he whispered so softly that Abigail strained to hear.

When he said nothing more immediately, Abigail nodded. "Anything."

"You agree without knowing exactly what my request entails?" David brushed his fingers along her cheek. "I want to marry you, my love."

"You do?" Abigail clenched his coat lapels to keep from falling. She had hoped but never dared let herself believe that he would propose today.

He cupped her face with both hands, smiling down on her with a wide grin. "I couldn't possibly have had any other thought in my mind after the events of the past few days. I should have explained myself better last night, but you've turned my world upside down and I must confess I like the confusion very much. I love you. Marry me. Come live with me in London and I promise to give you everything you need. My name. My boundless devotion. My every spare moment."

"Oh." Abigail's eyes filled with tears. He wanted to marry her.

She couldn't believe it really was happening. She closed her eyes to savor the moment and memorize how she felt. Having all your dreams come true was like spinning in the dark with only the bright moon to ground you. The tears fell down her cheeks, but she quickly blinked them away and raised her face in case he got the wrong idea of them.

David, however, frowned at something over the top of her head. "My love, I don't mean to be impatient, but I'll need an answer very soon. Your brother is about to come home and will not be happy to see us alone like this. Your reputation means everything to me."

He removed his hands from her face as the front door opened. He stepped back just as Peter reached the parlor doorway.

Peter blinked. "Hawke, what the devil are you doing here?"

When David glanced at her, she nodded quickly. "I will."

Peter approached, glancing between them. "What's going on? Have you been crying, Abigail?"

"Of course I have." She smiled at David. "I've just been made the happiest woman in Brighton. Mr. Hawke—David—has asked me to marry him and I've gladly accepted."

"Like hell you have." Her brother turned on David, fists clenched. "Haven't you caused enough trouble? You stay away from my sister."

"I cannot do that." David's gaze flicked in her direction, another smile broke free, making him appear so much happier than before. "I love her."

"Don't be ridiculous. You only love money."

David sighed, a little sadly. "I do love Abigail and cannot bear the thought of not seeing her every day."

Abigail caught David's hand and clung to his arm. "I feel exactly the same. Please be happy for me."

"Utterly out of the question," Peter snapped. "You'll be miserable and I'm putting a stop to this nonsense now before it goes too far." Then he stormed out of the house without another word or backwards glance.

"Now that reaction I hadn't considered," David muttered. He drew Abigail closer and pressed his head to hers. "My darling. My love. I'll convince him."

"How? He seems so set against the idea."

"Leave it to me." He twisted to kiss her cheek, and then brushed his lips softly against hers. "I'm not so easily put off as to believe his first answer. I count myself a skilled negotiator."

Abigail threw her arms around his neck, afraid to lose her chance at happiness. "Maybe he'll change his mind by the time you come back from London."

His arms tightened. "I'm not leaving Brighton until you're mine," he murmured against her ear. "Who knows what scandals you'll embark on if I'm not here to distract you?"

She laughed and drew him closer. "There is nothing to fear. I've saved all my scandalous plans for you."

David returned her embrace, his warm hands cradling her against him.

Afraid their time alone was short, she raised her head and kissed his lips hungrily, hoping to remind him of the passion they had shared last night and what was to come when they were married.

When he drew back, Abigail had successfully rumpled him.

"I should go before someone else walks in." He glanced around, guilt clear in his expression. "But hold onto that feeling until we're married. No more sneaking into my house."

Abigail pouted. "If you insist, but it will not be easy to stay away."

He kissed her again, a deep drugging kiss that went on and on. He lifted his head and began to laugh. "Abigail, what would I do without you? I am the luckiest of men, but I want everyone to know it before the next time you're in my bed for I doubt I'll let you out again."

Abigail laughed with him, but she also plotted her next scandalous adventure in his arms. The idea of never leaving his bed was *very* appealing.

Epilogue

———◆———

Waves crashed and fell in a steady rhythm along the shoreline of their swimming spot, but David didn't pay them any attention. His heart pulsed with a different rhythm now, part panic, part exhilaration. Abigail would be his wife. He just had to convince her stubborn brother it was in everyone's best interests without revealing the extent of the relationship. Abigail had already seduced him and he'd taken advantage of her too. There was only one course of action he could take. "I haven't changed my mind. I won't."

Beside him, Peter Watson let out an exaggerated huff. "How could you possibly marry her?"

"The better question is how could I not want to? She's lovely, sweet, intelligent, and makes me far happier than I've ever been. There is no one else."

And there never would be. He was quite certain it was Abigail or no one. He'd be a bachelor until his last breath without her.

The frown on Peter Watson's face grew. "She hasn't a penny."

David shook his head. "Money plays no part in this."

"It does for some of us," Peter said somewhat mulishly.

David sighed as he realized the real cause of Peter's objection. David wanted to marry Abigail because he loved her, whereas Peter would marry an heiress he didn't love for money. If David didn't know Miss George so well, he might have felt some pity for Peter. But Miss George was capable of great passion, as proved by her many stories. The man just needed to discover it for himself.

He tried another tack. "I understand you're surprised by this turn of events. In truth, I never imagined I would propose to Abigail when I first arrived in Brighton. But I love her and I will not leave without making her my wife. I've written my business partner and have taken leave from my duties in London until we are married."

Peter's eyes narrowed to slits. "You'd make that big a sacrifice?"

David worked to suppress a smile as he thought of last night. "Waiting for Abigail is no sacrifice."

"Hawke," Valentine Merton called.

David glanced behind and spotted his friend picking his way across the rocks to reach them. He waved. "Where have you been?"

"I was up late and slept late as a consequence." Valentine gave him an amused look. "Saw another fascinating constellation last night. It seems the night sky is growing more and more interesting every time I view it."

David suppressed a groan. Valentine had seen him and Abigail together again in the garden. "Never fear, I was just discussing the matter with Peter."

"Liar. We were not discussing the damn stars." Peter gestured at David angrily. "This fool thinks to wed my sister and I don't believe they'll suit."

"Congratulations, Hawke," Valentine said instantly, slapping David on the shoulder. "He's a lucky fellow, Watson, not a fool. Oh, and congratulations to you too. My sisters have just finished relaying the news that it's all set between you and Miss George. They say she is utterly delighted."

Peter scowled.

Valentine suddenly rubbed his hands together. "My, my, this has been an exciting time in Brighton. Two proposals in the same week, and one scandal in the wind."

David frowned. "A scandal?"

Valentine wagged his finger. "You'll have to stick around to find out. You miss out on so much by disappearing so quickly each year. A week is nowhere near long enough. Summer is a very exciting time to be in Brighton and this year seems to be the most promising."

"I'll be here," David assured him.

Peter scowled. "He'd better be here. I'm sure Abigail and Miss George are plotting a double wedding even as we speak."

David drew in a deep satisfied breath of sea air and then smiled. That was the yes he'd been waiting for all his life.

If you enjoyed Miss Watson's First Scandal
don't miss the next
Miss Mayhem romance

Miss George's Second Chance

Peter Watson had accepted that a loveless marriage was the only means to solve his financial problems until an unexpected inheritance changes everything. When Imogen releases him so he might marry for love instead, he discovers the carefree life of a peer lacks… the girl he never dared kiss.

About Heather Boyd

———◆———

Determined to escape the Aussie sun on a scorching camping holiday, Heather picked up a pen and notebook from a corner store and started writing her very first novel—Chills. Years later, she is the author of over thirty romances and has no plans to stop. Addicted to all things tech (never again will Heather write a novel longhand) and fascinated by English society of the early 1800's, Heather spends her days getting her characters in and out of trouble and into bed together (if they make it that far). She lives on the edge of beautiful Lake Macquarie, Australia with her trio of mischievous rogues (husband and two sons) along with one rescued cat whose only interest is that she provides him with food on demand.

You can find details of her writing at
www.Heather-Boyd.com